FORTUNES OF WAR

Since being orphaned, Lucy Prior has led a quiet life with her brother and his family on their farm in upstate New York. Now though, that peaceful existence is threatened by the approach of the American War of Independence. Even so, when she stumbles upon a handsome stranger hiding in the byre, Lucy cannot resist shielding him from his pursuers. But her actions will have far-reaching consequences — not only for herself, but also for the whole of her family.

JASMINA SVENNE

◆

FORTUNES OF WAR

Complete and Unabridged

LINFORD
Leicester

First published in Great Britain in 2009

First Linford Edition
published 2010

British Library CIP Data

Svenne, Jasmina M.
   Fortunes of war. - -
   (Linford romance library)
   1. New York (State)- -History- -Revolution,
   1775 – 1783- -Social aspects- -Fiction.
   2. Love stories. 3. Large type books.
   I. Title II. Series
   823.9'2–dc22

   ISBN 978–1–44480–184–2

Published by
F. A. Thorpe (Publishing)
Anstey, Leicestershire

Set by Words & Graphics Ltd.
Anstey, Leicestershire
Printed and bound in Great Britain by
T. J. International Ltd., Padstow, Cornwall

This book is printed on acid-free paper

1

'Is Robert not back yet from market?' The question greeted Lucy Prior as she entered the farmhouse and set down a pail of water. A long strand of golden brown hair had worked itself loose on her forehead and she pushed it out of her eyes with the back of her hand.

'I've not seen him anywhere in the yard,' she replied.

Abigail sighed and turned back to the bread oven to remove the last of this week's loaves.

'Well, I suppose it's not so very late yet.'

Lucy agreed as heartily as she could because she could see the disquiet in her sister-in-law's eyes.

It was still relatively early — it would not grow dark for at least another half an hour — but in these dangerous times, it was hard to know what was

1

normal and what a cause for alarm.

However, the two young women had a tacit agreement not to say anything that might upset the children and to confront any difficulties only when they arose.

'I suppose he'll have the latest news,' Lucy added, as cheerfully as possible. 'Perhaps that's what's keeping him. Maybe he met a friend just as he was setting out.'

'It wouldn't be the first time,' Abigail agreed and then turned towards little Robin, who was tugging at her skirts to attract her attention.

The baby started crying at the same moment, so Lucy picked her out of the wooden cradle and started jogging her up and down on her knee and rubbing her back.

'There now, sweetheart, Mamma will be here to feed you just as soon as she can,' she cooed, but for once her mind was not fully on the plight of her younger niece.

Once upon a time, Robert would

have been late coming home from Albany because someone had invited him to have a drink to celebrate the birth of a new child or the sale of a particularly profitable harvest, or even to sympathise with a bereavement.

But now the news was no longer about whose cattle had caught distemper or who had miraculously recovered from a life-threatening illness. A new threat was seeping closer, one for which they could not prepare because they had no idea if it would reach them and if so, in what way.

'Someone's coming,' six-year-old Jenny exclaimed. She had been shelling peas and now leapt to her feet so suddenly that she knocked the bowl, causing a fountain of peas to spray up in the air and across the table.

Lucy put Caroline back in the cradle, intending to help her sister-in-law, but Abigail brushed her away.

'I'll see to this,' she said. 'You go with the children.'

Jenny had already managed to reach

the latch and yank the door open and her little brother was not far behind.

Lucy did as Abigail had asked. In the days before the war, neither of them would have had any qualms about letting the children dash out like this at the sound of hooves, knowing that it was most likely a passing neighbour.

Now there was no saying who it might be — Continental militia or regular army, northern families displaced from their farmsteads by the approach of war, recruits on their way to Stillwater, even the dreaded Indians or deserters or other ne'er-do-wells that profited from other people's misery.

'Papa, Papa!' both children chorused and Lucy let out a sigh of relief.

Then she caught sight of her brother's face. There was suppressed excitement in his eyes, perhaps agitation or even anger. But he made an effort to control himself for the sake of his children.

'And how are my little ruffians?' Robert asked, swinging down from high

4

up in his saddle.

'We're not ruffians,' Jenny declared. 'We've been ever so good. I fed the chickens all by myself.'

'Did you bring us something nice?' Robin chimed in.

Robert laughed. 'I might have done. You'll have to wait and see. I don't give presents to children who don't kiss their poor old papa.'

In normal circumstances, Lucy would have left Robert with the children and returned to the farmhouse to help Abigail. But she sensed something was wrong, so she stayed to watch the children hug their father and raid one of the deep pockets of his frockcoat for a twist of paper containing a stick of peppermint for each of them.

'Now you run along inside and show your mother,' Robert said, tapping each of them lightly on the bottom.

They scampered off, crying out to their mother, leaving the two adults in the yard. Robert made as if to lead his horse to the stable, but Lucy stopped him in his tracks.

'What's wrong?' she asked.

He gave her a sharp look. 'Why should anything be wrong?'

Lucy shook her head. 'You can't pull the wool over my eyes, Bob,' she said. 'I know you too well. Something happened while you were in town, or there's news about the war or something.'

He glanced at her, then at the farmhouse.

'I really ought to tell Abigail first,' he said.

Lucy's heart sank. Then something really was wrong.

'You do understand . . . ' Robert began.

'Yes, yes, of course. Abigail has first claim. Only — I was rather hoping you'd tell me I'd been imagining things.'

Robert grinned unexpectedly.

'I could still tell you that,' he offered, 'but would you believe me?'

'I'm afraid not.' Lucy laughed.

And so they went their separate ways to continue with all their evening chores that had to be done.

'I don't know what Robert is thinking, wasting money we don't have on sweet things for the children,' Abigail remarked as Lucy entered, but the words were spoken with affectionate exasperation. 'I've a good mind to give him a piece of my mind.'

'Perhaps you should go and talk to him,' Lucy suggested. 'There may be news he'd rather not talk about in front of the children. I'll finish up in here for you.'

Abigail looked as if she was going to object. Then she took a closer look at Lucy's grave expression and nodded.

'I might well do that.'

Lucy persuaded the children to lay the table while she dished up the hot food. A glance out of the window showed her that Robert and Abigail were apparently in deep conversation. Robert had temporarily slung his saddlebags over the fence so he wouldn't have to hold them. The conversation was clearly growing passionate. Abigail's voice had become high and shrill. Lucy noticed both of the older children had grown alert and were glancing towards the door.

'Is Mamma cross about Papa buying us presents?' Jenny asked.

'No, no, I'm sure she's not cross at all. And even if she is, it has nothing to do with you. Now, who is going to help me tidy up so there is more room for the things Papa bought at market?'

Though Lucy spoke cheerfully to the children, her heart misgave her. It was quite out of character for Abigail to be angry with Robert. On the whole, the two of them rubbed along admirably, Abigail's calmness acting as a brake on Robert's more impetuous nature. Lucy had often thought that if she could find someone whose sense of humour and values matched her own as well as Robert's did with Abigail's, she would have a very happy marriage.

The thought of marriage was never

very far from Lucy's mind these days. She was grateful to Robert and Abigail for taking her in after her father had died two years previously, leaving her homeless. She had done her best to repay their generosity by making herself useful about the farm and taking care of Jenny and Robin while Abigail was pregnant with and recovering from the birth of Caroline. She knew that, if she had not been there, either Abigail would have had to manage on her own, with occasional help from their nearest neighbours, or Robert would have had to spend money he could not afford hiring a servant.

But there were times when Lucy felt like a spare limb at the farm, when Robert and Abigail might have preferred a little privacy. The older the children grew, the more they would be able to help around the farm, making Lucy redundant. She did not want to stay there forever as a poor relation. And it would be nice to have a home of her own, even if it was only a tiny shack in the depths of the dark forests.

The trouble was that the Priors' farm was in such an isolated part of upstate New York, Lucy met very few unmarried men and so far none of those she had met had ignited a spark in the hidden depths of her heart, though she had had one or two offers of marriage.

The door opened just as everything was ready indoors and Lucy had begun to wonder whether it was a good idea to venture outside to summon the others to supper before it got cold.

Abigail was looking distinctly tight-lipped as she took her place at the table and began dissecting a rabbit pie. Robert left the saddlebags to one side, to be unpacked later, and hastily washed his hands.

He chattered cheerfully enough about trivial things, to mask the general air of unease, and thankfully Jenny and Robin responded to him and seemed not to notice that their mother was preoccupied and their aunt bewildered.

What could Robert have told Abigail

that could discompose her so much? As a rule nothing seemed to ruffle her for long.

Lucy managed to rein in her curiosity until the children were all safely tucked up in bed and the three adults were alone.

'Now,' Lucy said, 'would somebody please tell me what on earth is going on?'

Abigail and Robert exchanged looks. They had sat down on either side of the table, instead of moving closer to the hearth, as they would have done in normal circumstances. Lucy shivered, but it had nothing to do with the autumnal chill in the air.

'It seems your precious brother has put all he claims to hold dear at risk by openly declaring his loyalty to the Crown,' Abigail replied in very clipped tones.

'Oh.' Lucy was taken somewhat aback. Ever since hostilities broke out some two years previously between the British authorities and the American rebels, the Priors had tried to remain neutral. If anything they leaned towards the side of King George III and his representatives, since the taxes objected to by American merchants and politicians had long since been repealed and, as Robert said, there was far less danger of being tyrannised by a king across the vast stretch of the Atlantic Ocean than by some jumped-up turkey-cock living in the nearest town.

As if to prove this point, Lucy had read some sickening accounts in the newspapers of Tory-baiting, in which people who claimed to be in favour of liberty and free speech had cruelly mistreated others for holding a contrary opinion to their own or, in the case of excise officers, simply for attempting to carry out the duties for which they were paid.

'What exactly happened?' she asked now.

Abigail allowed Robert to tell the story. It seemed he had stopped to drink a mug of ale before leaving

Albany, but had wound up intervening in a drunken brawl in which another man had been attacked by several others for refusing to drink a toast to General Washington. If Robert had left it at that, all might still have ended well. But he had unwisely made a few sharp comments of his own.

'You wouldn't have me go against my principles, would you?' Robert challenged his wife.

'Yes. No. I don't know any more. All I want is for the Whigs to leave us alone, allow us to farm our little bit of land and most of all, let me bring up my children in peace and security.'

'And what peace and security is there for us, now the war is creeping ever closer? There has already been one battle near Saratoga — that's scarcely a day's journey from here. How long do you think it will be before we are pulled into the midst of all this?'

Abigail leaned both elbows on the table so she could hide her face deep in her hands.

13

'Is it really that bad?' Lucy asked, putting a hand on her sister-in-law's shoulder, but looking across the table at her brother.

'Yes, I'm afraid it is.'

Since midsummer, the British army with its German and Canadian allies had been working its way down from Lake Champlain. Fort Ticonderoga had been abandoned by the Americans without a fight, but several battles and skirmishes had occurred along the route southwards, though the precise details seemed to differ in every account Lucy had heard or read.

But on the whole, the general agreement was that things did not look good for the British under General Burgoyne, unless help came from the south from General Clinton in New York, or General Carleton in Quebec sent substantial reinforcements.

'I'm sorry if I've upset you, Abigail,' Robert went on, 'and I am sorry if I have put you and Lucy and the children in any danger. But if I had been a single man with no responsibilities, I would have enlisted long ago.'

'I didn't know you felt that way,' Abigail said stiffly and Lucy knew she was close to tears.

'No, well, there was nothing I could do about it, and if circumstances had not provoked me, I might have bitten my tongue. But my pride as a man wouldn't let me keep silent any longer. I felt like a coward and a hypocrite, as if I was simply waiting to see which side will win before pandering to the victor in the hopes of some lucrative reward. You do understand, don't you?'

Abigail lifted her head and Lucy could see she looked worn out from emotion, hard work and sleepless nights with the baby.

'Yes, I understand. I even forgive you. Nay more, I'm proud of you, for standing up to the mob like that. But, oh, how I wish this war was over and none of this would be necessary.'

★ ★ ★

The light was not yet strong the following morning when Lucy and Abigail let the cows out of the byre to be milked. It was early in the year to be locking the cattle away for the night — only the beginning of October — but Robert had thought the precaution justified. Not only were there bears and wolves in the forest, but desperate men too.

The job did not take long. Already the yields were decreasing and the milk itself no longer as creamy as during the bright days of late spring and early summer. Lucy tried singing under her breath to put the cows at ease, but today they seemed strangely restless.

'There, that's the last of them,' she said, rising from her stool and stretching her back. 'If you take my pail, I'll let them into the meadow and start on the mucking out.'

'Are you sure?' Abigail asked, taking the second pail nonetheless. 'I seem to remember you did the mucking out yesterday too.'

'I'm sure. I need a bit of fresh air to clear my head and the walk will do me good.'

The truth was that Lucy had not slept well and she suspected the more skilled task of skimming the cream from the surface of the milk for butter and cheese might be beyond her this morning.

Abigail made no further objection and the two young women went about their business. It promised to be a clear, cold day, the morning haze already beginning to dissipate.

On her way back from the pasture, Lucy collected the wheelbarrow and a shovel. It was dark inside the byre in contrast with the daylight outside, apart from a rectangular patch near the door. Something rustled in the straw, but Lucy scarcely noticed. Mice and rats were common enough, despite their best efforts.

Then she froze. Was she imagining things? Or could she hear someone or something breathing rapidly close by?

17

She swung round, overwhelmed by a sudden presentiment of danger.

A gasp escaped her. There, pressed flat against the wall of the byre, was a tall, dark figure. There wasn't even time for her to cry out. Before she could flee, a large hand had grabbed hold of her arm and flung her against the wall, while another hand pressed firmly across her mouth.

2

'Please don't be alarmed,' a low, masculine voice breathed in her face. 'I mean you no harm. If you will just let me shelter in your byre until nightfall, I'll be on my way.'

The stranger towered over her, but although his grip was firm, it was not painful. Lucy looked up into his face and noted his strong, clearly defined features. A faint suspicion of stubble dappled his jaw and his dark hair was clubbed at the back of his neck in a military fashion. But it was his eyes that arrested her, gleaming earnestly at her through the half-light.

He allowed Lucy to push his hand away from her mouth.

'Who are you?' she whispered, her mind whirring. Robert was already out in the fields, examining a damaged boundary fence, while Abigail was in

19

the house with the children. Would anyone hear her if she screamed? Should she use the shovel as a weapon? Or would the stranger be revenged on her long before anyone could come to her assistance?

Perhaps instead she could lull him into inattention and then flee, locking him inside the byre until she could fetch her brother and the gun. She shuddered to think how vulnerable they would have been if this man had come the previous day, while Robert was away.

'I'm sorry. I can't tell you that,' the stranger replied, 'but I swear I won't hurt you.'

He released her arm and took a step back. Lucy peeked at the open door out of the corner of her eye. Could she reach the yard if she made a run for it? He was still perilously close.

'Why should I trust you?'

He shook his head. 'I can't think of a single reason why you should,' he admitted. 'Please, I wouldn't ask such a favour in ordinary circumstances, but it's a matter of life and death. And you may be my only hope right now.'

She could hear the desperation in his well-bred voice and she found herself wavering, despite her better judgement. But before she could reply, a rough voice called from outside, startling them both.

'Hey there! Anyone home?'

Reacting faster than the stranger, Lucy shoved him aside and rushed to the open door. There she came to a halt.

A motley group of men, wearing Continental Militia uniforms and bearing flintlocks, were clustered near the farmyard gate. Lucy recognised some faces as belonging to local men, though there were none she knew well.

'What is it?'

Her voice did not sound like her own, but no one seemed to notice.

'Nearly caught a damned enemy spy,' one of the men called back and spat heartily. 'You seen which way he went?

He had clubbed hair and a blue coat.'

She couldn't help but be aware of the man pressed against the wall of the byre behind her and the temptation to glance back, just to gauge his reaction, was almost irresistible.

'Blue coat and clubbed hair?' she repeated and sensed the man behind her stiffening. Silently she prayed he wouldn't react too soon.

'That's right.'

'I think I saw someone like that heading towards the river.'

Her heart beat tumultuously. Would they believe her?

'Villain must have doubled back on himself,' one of the men muttered.

And then, to her amazement, they called out their thanks and headed off in the direction she had indicated. Only when they were out of sight and earshot did she dare look back at the stranger.

'They've gone,' she said.

'Thank you. I cannot begin to express how grateful I am . . . '

'Aye, well.' Lucy shrugged, suddenly

abashed. The stranger had clasped her hand in a warm, strong grip. 'They've hanged two of the king's officers already as spies. I'd rather not have a third on my conscience.'

The stranger parted his lips, as if to deny he was a British officer. But Lucy saw the dark cloud pass over his eyes. The deaths of those other men in such ignominious circumstances clearly troubled him.

Instead all he said was, 'War is an ugly business.'

For a moment they were both silent. Lucy began to back away self-consciously before another thought struck her.

'Come on,' she said. 'You'll be safer and more comfortable in the hayloft.'

She led the way up the ladder. The hayloft above the byre was still pretty full, as it was early in the season, but between the two of them, they moved some of the hay to create a narrow space for him behind a protective parapet.

'I really ought to be getting back to

work now,' she whispered when they were done. 'My sister-in-law will be wondering what is taking me so long.'

'Of course. I'm sorry to be such a burden.'

Lucy was about to scramble down when one final thought struck her.

'Do you need food?'

The man hesitated. 'Only if you can spare it. I'll pay for it, naturally.'

If she had had any doubts that he was a British or Loyalist officer, that offer would have dispelled them. The Continentals or patriots — whichever name they called themselves — never seemed to have any money and grabbed and demanded whatever they wanted, making vague promises about Congress reimbursing farmers for their losses by and by.

'I'll see what I can find.'

She had not yet decided if she ought to tell Abigail or Robert about the stranger. It was not that she didn't trust them, but the fewer people that knew, the better. And yet how else would she explain the disappearance of much-needed food? She couldn't deprive the children of their due share. No, anything she did save for the stranger would have to come out of her own portion.

'Wait!'

The whisper halted her again, half-way down the ladder.

'What is it?'

The stranger's face appeared above the parapet of hay.

'Would you mind telling me your name, so I know who I am indebted to?'

Lucy hesitated, but she couldn't see any harm in telling him.

'Lucy Prior. And yours?'

He hesitated even longer and Lucy realised how much danger he would put himself into if he told her the truth and she betrayed him.

'Selbourne,' he said. 'Joseph Selbourne.'

★   ★   ★

'You've been a long time,' Abigail remarked as her sister-in-law slipped into the farmhouse.

Lucy blushed guiltily. 'Oh, well — there was a group of militia looking for a man,' she replied, trying to keep her voice vague. She was sure that somebody had told her once that clever liars stuck as closely as they could to the truth. 'They went off in the direction of the river, I think.'

Abigail tutted and shook her head. 'I don't like this at all. The war is getting a deal too close.'

Lucy felt it safer not to reply. She was busily calculating how she could pocket half her breakfast for Selbourne and how quickly she could get him away from the farm. Dusk seemed such a long way away. At least at this time of year, there would be little occasion for anyone to venture into the hayloft before evening — but that included herself. If she was caught going in or out, questions might be asked.

Breakfast provided the perfect opportunity to ask Robert and Abigail what work they had planned for the day and where they wanted her help. It gave her a better idea when the farmyard was likely to be empty, so she could slip away unnoticed.

This proved to be easier than she had anticipated since the entire family spent the best part of the day in the orchard, gathering the remaining apples and pears. Even Jenny and Robin helped where they could and when the first of the large panniers were full, Lucy offered to take the fruit to the house and check on Caroline, who had been left sleeping in her cradle in the farmhouse because it was too cold for her outdoors.

She carried out the tasks she had undertaken first. It was easy enough to slip an apple into her apron pocket alongside the hunk of bread and cheese she had saved from breakfast. At the last moment, she decided to take a mug of small ale as well. Then she crept up to the hayloft as carefully as she could.

Before she was halfway up the ladder, she could hear soft, deep breathing. Cautiously she squeezed through the wall of hay before being brought to a standstill. Selbourne was curled up on one side, his cheek pillowed on his hand, fast asleep. Lucy couldn't help thinking how young and vulnerable he looked, no more than perhaps four or five years older than herself. There were dark shadows under his eyes, as if he had been deprived of sleep for far too long.

Perhaps it was as well not to disturb him. She placed the food, wrapped in a clean handkerchief, to one side of him, where she hoped he would find it before the rats did. She looked round for something to cover the mug, to prevent dust and rubbish from falling into it. In the end she had to content herself with using the handkerchief that was tied around her shoulders because there was nothing else remotely suitable.

Selbourne stirred as she was about to descend, and she was both relieved and disappointed when he did not wake. But she could not afford to wait. The others would miss her and there was plenty of work to be done.

She had not quite reached the ground, however, when a loud cry from the farmyard made her start.

'Miss Prior? Are you there?'

The familiar voice filled Lucy's heart with dread. Isaac Wilcox. What on earth could bring him here at this hour? She scrambled down the ladder as quickly and quietly as she could, but she was too late. As she turned, she found a figure in militia uniform standing a few feet away from her.

'What on earth are you doing here, Miss Prior? Your sister said you'd be in the apple loft.'

Lucy saw Isaac Wilcox's eyes slide involuntarily from her face to the square neck of her bodice, which had been left more exposed than usual by the absence of her handkerchief.

Lucy forced an unconvincing smile to her lips.

'I thought I heard something, but it must have been just rats,' she said.

She knew she had to get Wilcox away from the byre as quickly as possible, in case their voices woke Selbourne, or Wilcox volunteered to investigate the noises in the hayloft himself.

'What brings you here?' she added hurriedly, but Wilcox ignored her question.

'You ought to be more careful. There's desperate characters around in this area.' He nodded up towards the hayloft. 'You want me to go and take a look?'

'No, no, I've already done it. It's only rats.' Lucy knew she was talking much too fast and betraying her uneasiness. Instinctively she had grasped Wilcox's arm to detain him as he attempted to push past her. 'I ought to get back to the orchard.'

'Just one moment. I wanted to speak to you about what happened this morning.'

Lucy's heart beat so hard against her stays, she was surprised the whole farmyard did not echo with the sound.

'This morning?' she faltered.

'My men tell me you saw someone hereabouts.'

Something stirred in the hay overhead and it took a conscious effort not to glance up. What if Selbourne was waking? Or what if he snored or talked in his sleep? Please God, don't let him do anything that would betray his presence.

'I don't know what I can tell you,' she said, raising her voice a little. 'It was only a vague figure in the distance — it might not even be the man you are looking for.'

'Well, that's a shame. I was hoping perhaps you might have remembered a little more about him — like precisely where he was heading. Only my men couldn't find a trace of him, nor any other witnesses.'

Why, oh why had she said anything at all? Lucy groaned inwardly. It would have been so much easier for everyone concerned if she had told the militiamen that she had seen no one and let them go on their way. Only she had been afraid they might have wanted to search the farmyard and outbuildings.

'I'm sorry I can't be of more use,' she said and attempted to slip past him.

This time it was his turn to catch her by the arm.

'What's your hurry?' he asked. 'Your brother and sister know I wanted a word with you.' His leer widened and again his eyes dropped. They were standing so close together, Lucy knew he could see the curve of her breasts behind the low neckline of her gown.

'You know, it could be to your advantage to be nicer to me,' he added, leaning closer so she could smell onions on his breath. 'Things are looking pretty bad for Burgoyne's troops and I hear your brother isn't making things easy for himself. Could be there'll be a time soon when you'll be glad of a friend on the winning side.'

So that was what this was all about, Lucy thought. Isaac Wilcox had proposed marriage to her some months ago. She had turned him down, not only because she was indifferent towards him as a person, but because from some inadvertent words he had let slip during the proposal, she had deduced that his chief interest in her lay in her skills as a potential housekeeper and agricultural labourer for the property he owned on the other side of the parish. Or perhaps she had been mistaken about that.

'The winning side?' Lucy echoed, lifting her chin a little higher. 'Correct me if I'm wrong, but I heard that General Howe has driven General Washington out of Philadelphia. Surely that means the war isn't over yet — nor entirely one-sided?'

Wilcox flushed with annoyance. Lucy tried to yank her arm free, but he only tightened his grip.

'Philadelphia is a long way away from here,' he muttered thickly. 'How is

Howe going to help you now?'

Before Lucy had a chance to respond, his hand had clamped on the back of her head and he had forced a clumsy kiss on her lips.

Revulsion gave Lucy unsuspected strength. She pushed his face away from hers with both hands. She had always thought Isaac Wilcox harmless enough, until he had joined the militia as an officer, because he had enough influence to buy himself rank over poorer neighbours. Now the power seemed to have gone to his head.

'Oh fie, Mr Wilcox, I thought it was only licentious British soldiers who took advantage of poor, innocent country girls like me,' Lucy mocked, making her eyes wide and child-like.

She had heard ominous rustling in the hayloft above and was almost convinced that Selbourne was awake and tempted to fly to her rescue, an action that might make things ten times worse for all of them in the long term.

'I've asked you to marry me like an

honest man,' Wilcox muttered sullenly.

'Yes, but I believe I gave you my answer long ago and I'm quite certain I haven't changed my mind meanwhile,' she retorted.

Wilcox stared at Lucy mutinously, obviously annoyed that he could not find a witty enough retort to fire back at her.

'You're mighty proud for somebody who has nothing,' he said, picking a stray strand of hay out of Lucy's hair. 'Just you be careful you don't come to rue spurning my help one of these days.'

And with that he turned on his heel and strode off across the yard.

3

It was dusk before Lucy dared venture back to the hayloft. It had been incredibly tempting to scramble up there as soon as Wilcox was out of sight, because she wanted to talk to someone about what had just happened. But it was not impossible that Wilcox had found himself a convenient hiding place in the nearby forest so he could watch if she would lead him directly to the fugitive.

Besides which, Lucy knew she had been away from the orchard far too long and the others would be growing concerned. Abigail in particular noticed that she was flustered when she returned. Lucy fended off her questions as best she could.

'You should have told me you saw a stranger this morning.'

Lucy flushed. 'Yes, well, I — I didn't

want to alarm you. And I only caught a glimpse from a distance. It might not even have been the man the militia are looking for.'

She was still upset about Wilcox's kiss and was tempted to tell Abigail everything, but just at that moment Robin tripped over a gnarled tree root and set up a howl that only his mother could soothe.

I have to get Selbourne away tonight, Lucy thought, stretching up for an apple that was almost out of reach. It's the only way to keep us all safe.

With that in mind, she set about planning what food she could collect that wouldn't be missed. She had no idea if Selbourne was heading north or south, but she guessed she would have to give him some directions to help him on his way.

It took her three attempts to reach the hayloft safely. Every time she approached it, either Robert or Abigail would appear from somewhere and she would have to pretend she was carrying out some other errand, like shutting the chickens up for the night or going to the dairy to skim off the cream from the evening's milk. And just as she finally managed to reach the top of the ladder, she heard the gate creak and hooves thud across the yard.

'It's only me,' she whispered, squeezing into the narrow hollow they had created for Selbourne. 'We have to be quiet, though — there's someone below.'

Selbourne had obviously heard her coming because he was kneeling at the far end of the hollow, his right hand stretched towards his left side, as if he was reaching for his sword or a pistol. At the sight of her, his arm dropped to his side and his face relaxed into a smile.

'I'm glad to see you,' he said. 'That brute earlier on — he didn't hurt or frighten you, did he?'

'Who? Isaac Wilcox? No, he didn't hurt me.'

She had not had much time to dwell

on Wilcox's words or actions since she resumed work, but she realised that Selbourne had had nothing to occupy his mind in the intervening hours, apart from planning the next stage of his journey and brooding about the conversation he must have overheard.

'Good. You have no notion how close I came to doing something rash.' Selbourne seemed abashed by his own vehemence and he looked away. 'I suppose I have you to thank for this?' he asked.

He held out the tankard and the handkerchiefs. Lucy flushed, remembering how she had watched him sleeping.

'Yes. I've brought you some more food. It isn't much, but I hope it will be better than nothing.'

She fumbled in her pocket for another hunk of bread and cheese, an apple and — her greatest triumph — a narrow sliver of cold rabbit pie left over from the previous night, wrapped in a piece of brown paper.

'You've been more than generous. Here, you must let me pay you for my board and lodgings.'

It took some negotiating before they could agree. If nothing else, Lucy felt bad about accepting money for food that she supposed she had really stolen from her brother.

'Please take it,' Selbourne urged. 'You never know when it might come in useful, especially while the situation is so unsettled.'

'Very well,' Lucy agreed reluctantly, resolving privately not to spend the money until she could buy something useful for the farm, or perhaps a little treat for the children.

'I suppose I ought to be going,' Selbourne said. 'Is it quite dark yet?'

'Not quite. You'd better let me go first, to make sure the coast is clear. Which way are you going — north or south?'

Selbourne shook his head. 'I can't tell you that.'

'Surely you can trust me after

everything that happened this morning?'

'It's not that. It would be safer for you to know as little as possible.'

'Yes, but how can I give you any directions unless I know where you are headed?'

Still he hesitated. He isn't going to tell me, Lucy thought.

'Northward,' he said at last. 'But don't ask me any more.'

Northward. He was trying to get to Burgoyne's beleaguered army, that much was evident, presumably with a coded message from Clinton, or even Howe, hidden somewhere on his person.

Lucy said no more. Instead she scrambled down the ladder. The yard appeared to be deserted and the twilight was thickening, assisted by a heavy pall of cloud that might well bring rain. She was about to knock the all-clear signal they had agreed upon when a little voice piped up.

'Aunt Lucy? Mamma wants you.'

41

Flushed and overheated, Lucy turned. She had not spotted Jenny in the shadow of the hen coop.

'Tell your mamma I'm coming. There's something I need to do first.'

The little girl ran off without complaint. Lucy gave the signal and a moment later Selbourne had landed softly beside her. Her heart in her throat, she guided him round the back of the outbuildings, where they were less likely to be seen from the farmhouse.

'Are you sure you must go now?' she asked in a whisper, glancing up at the tumultuous sky. 'It looks like there'll be a downpour in less than an hour.'

'The longer I stay, the more peril I put you in, and the rest of your family. Besides, I've a long way to go and I fear time is growing short. I can't afford to waste hours in which my pursuers could conceivably be taking shelter.'

Selbourne slipped through a gate in the fence, but when Lucy made as if to follow, he stopped her.

'I don't think you should come any further,' he said. 'It might not be safe for a woman on her own when you come to return home.'

Lucy parted her lips to protest that she had often gone out at even later, darker hours, but then she closed her mouth again. These were not ordinary circumstances and she knew there were bears and wolves in the forest, even without newer dangers.

'Very well,' she said and proceeded to give him as many directions as she could to guide him onward.

'I cannot thank you enough for your kindness,' Selbourne said, offering her his hand.

She slipped her hand into his and to her surprise, instead of merely shaking it, he lifted it to his lips and kissed it.

'Farewell. I'll never forget you.'

Before Lucy could recover, he had set off at a brisk pace through the trees. She wanted to call goodbye to him, but common sense told her that she ought to remain quiet so as not to draw unwanted attention to either of them. She cradled her hand against her breast. Her skin still tingled with the imprint of Selbourne's kiss and it almost surprised her that it had left no mark.

She had intended to go straight back to the house, but a thought struck her as she passed the hayloft. She climbed up the ladder one last time. As she had suspected, Selbourne had not had enough time to obliterate the traces of his hiding place. The empty hollow among the hay was still visible.

Lucy was half-tempted to leave it as it was, to provide herself with a sanctuary if ever she needed to be on her own with her thoughts, but she knew it was too dangerous. There must be no sign that anything unusual had happened, especially if Isaac Wilcox was suspicious.

She rearranged the hay, then climbed down the ladder. Before she faced Abigail and Robert, she wanted to splash her face with water from the well, though she had to dry herself on her own apron.

As she opened the door, she heard Jenny's crystal clear voice, obviously defending herself. 'I don't know what she was doing. All she said was that she was coming soon.'

'I'm sorry I took so long, Abigail. I had to . . . ' But her hastily concocted excuse died on her lips.

The family was not alone. There was a man sitting beside Robert by the fire. His head whipped round at the sound of her voice so he could give her a penetrating stare. Lucy jumped so violently, the pewter tankard she had been hiding behind her petticoats slipped from her grasp with a clatter. It rolled across the floor and came to a rest at the feet of Isaac Wilcox.

Lucy's breath caught at the top of her throat. For a second she was paralysed. Then she dived forward to retrieve the incriminating item, but she was too late. Isaac Wilcox had already bent down and their heads collided with a shock that made them both gasp in pain. Still, Lucy managed to snatch the tankard first, even if she could not conceal from Wilcox what it was.

'Where on earth did that come from?' Abigail asked, baffled, when she saw what Lucy was holding.

'I — I must have knocked it down from — from the table or — or a shelf in passing,' Lucy stammered, but her voice sounded as breathless as she felt. She lifted her free hand to her throbbing forehead and blinked back tears of pain.

She expected Wilcox to contradict her, but instead she saw a cunning gleam appear in his eyes, which did nothing to calm her nerves.

'Well, never mind that now,' Robert said. 'Lieutenant Wilcox wanted to ask you if you'd seen any more of that stranger, or remembered some other detail about him.'

Lucy shook her head. Her heartbeat was still much faster than it ought to have been and she didn't trust her voice. But she had to make an effort, to buy Selbourne some time to get clear of the farm. She was painfully aware of how close he must still be, even if he had managed to keep up his swift pace amid the obstacles of the darkening forest.

'Surely he must be far away from here by now — halfway to Albany or Saratoga, or wherever he was heading,' she forced herself to say, but her voice came out choked and unnatural.

It frightened her that it must have been Wilcox she had heard arriving as she scrambled into the hayloft. If luck had not been on their side, she and Selbourne might have encountered him in the yard.

'No doubt you're right, Miss Prior,' Wilcox said, not taking his eyes off her face for a second. 'It's just that I worry about your family's safety — two women and three children with only one man to protect you.'

Lucy sensed a second, more sinister

meaning beneath his seemingly innocent words.

'I'm sure we're all very grateful for your concern,' she replied, a little too stiffly to be convincing.

Would it be a good idea to keep Wilcox here as long as possible, to give Selbourne a better chance of making his escape? Or could she persuade him by her behaviour that the British officer was still hidden somewhere nearby? While she was still hesitating, she heard the first raindrops patter against the windowpane.

'Looks like we'll have quite a shower,' Abigail said. 'Why don't you stay and sup with us, Mr Wilcox? There's enough to go round.'

Isaac Wilcox had never been a particular favourite of hers and she knew he was one of Lucy's rejected suitors, but clearly Abigail felt that in these dangerous times, it might be as well not to make unnecessary enemies.

Wilcox glanced at Lucy to gauge her reaction, but she deliberately turned away to stir the vegetable stew that was bubbling over the fire. Secretly she was relieved. Given their earlier exchange, it was far more natural that the invitation had come from Abigail. Robert too did a good job of persuading their unexpected guest to stay.

'Well, when you ask me so kindly, how can I say no?' Wilcox replied and Lucy sensed that he was still watching her. 'It's been a while since I've tasted anything that smelt half so good.'

He wants to catch me out, Lucy thought. He thinks the longer he stays here, the more likely I am to betray myself. Well, let him stay. He won't see anything and it will buy Selbourne more time. That is, unless he runs into some kind of patrol or foraging party along the way.

The atmosphere during supper was strained. At every rattle of the wind, Lucy stole a glance at the door, terrified that Wilcox's underlings might burst in triumphantly with the news that they had caught their quarry. Moreover,

Isaac Wilcox sat directly opposite to Lucy and she was acutely aware that he was watching every little thing she did.

'You're very quiet tonight, Lucy,' Robert remarked.

It took her a moment to realise her brother had been speaking to her.

'What? Oh, I suppose I'm just tired after all the harvesting. Still, at least it's nearly over and we'll be snug for the winter.' She mustered a smile, but she wasn't sure anyone was convinced by it.

At long last the interminable meal was over. Isaac Wilcox finally pushed back the bench and stood up to leave. He thanked Robert and Abigail for their hospitality, but while Lucy gathered up the platters and cutlery, she could feel his eyes still upon her.

'I wondered, Miss Prior, if I could have one word with you in private?'

Lucy's heart jolted so hard, it almost winded her. The last thing she wanted was yet another tussle with Isaac Wilcox. But if she did not go outside with him, he might decide to spy round the farmyard on his own.

'I'll walk you to the gate,' she said.

She wrapped herself in her cloak, pulled the hood well forward and took a lantern to light the way.

'Well, what is it?' she demanded as soon as the door had closed behind them.

Wilcox made her wait. He fussed round his horse, tightening its girth, stroking its muzzle and generally paying far more heed to it than he did to the young woman beside him.

'I thought you might have changed your mind,' he said, without turning his head in her direction.

'About what? Marrying you?'

'You could do worse. I've a good bit of property crying out for an able mistress like you. And I'm likely to be promoted in the militia too, as soon as there are any vacancies.'

Lucy did not reply.

'No, I never had too many hopes that way,' Wilcox said after a moment, turning towards her at last, 'but I did

51

think you'd be sensible enough to do the right thing to help your brother and his family. Are you sure there's not something troubling your conscience? Some little thing you might confess to me, quite privately, mind, so I could make all your troubles melt away.'

'Such as?' Lucy asked, her mouth dry.

'Such as the hiding place of a certain English spy.'

'I don't know what you're talking about.' Lucy lifted her head higher and in the darkness, she hoped he could not see her lips quiver.

'Pity,' Wilcox remarked, giving her one last look. 'I would've liked to help you if I could.'

With that he fitted his foot in his stirrup, hauling himself into the saddle.

4

The parting words of Isaac Wilcox stayed with Lucy. She tried to convince herself that the worst that could happen if Wilcox betrayed her was that the Continental Army might come and search the farm.

She slept badly and spent the next morning in a state of alert, waiting for something to happen. And yet when it did, she was strangely unprepared.

It started out as a perfectly ordinary day. Afterwards Lucy remembered feeling a vague sense of emptiness, now Selbourne was gone. He had been on her mind so much during the previous day, she found it difficult to believe that he had been there for such a short time.

She was in the yard at about midday, hauling a bucket of water from the well, when she heard the distant thunder of hooves. For a moment she froze, her head raised to listen. Could the militia be on its way to the farmstead?

Then she shook herself. It would be far better if she got into the house, out of sight, before the patrol arrived, so she would not have to face them alone. The hooves sounded ominously close now. She grasped the handle of the bucket with both hands to help her bear its weight.

But she was not fast enough. She had not yet reached the house when she heard the hooves stop at the gate. A masculine voice called out.

'Hey there, is Mr Robert Prior about?'

Dread gripped Lucy's stomach as she turned towards the speaker. He was rough-looking and unshaven and she flinched from his lecherous gaze. But what horrified her most was the sheer number of his followers. She had never seen such a large body of Continental Militia, except at drills and reviews in town.

This can't be good, a voice whispered

in her ear. Either they had come for Selbourne, or else Robert's indiscreet words at Albany had been taken note of and had imperilled them all.

'What's wrong, sweetheart? Cat got your tongue?' the same speaker sneered.

'I — I'm not sure where my brother is,' she replied, but her voice sounded husky. It was not strictly a lie. Robert might have been in any number of places, in the fields or the orchard or one of the outbuildings.

A sound distracted her. The farm-house door had opened and Abigail appeared, the baby in the crook of her arm, the older children clinging to her petticoats.

'Morning, ma'am,' the sergeant raised his hat a fraction. 'We're looking for your husband.'

'What do you want with him?' Abigail asked. Her voice was steady, but Lucy saw her knuckles whiten as she pressed Caroline tighter to her breast.

'You'll find out soon enough when we find him.'

They were flooding into the farmyard now.

'He's not here. He went to — to town,' Lucy blurted out.

'Is that a fact? Then why is his horse still in the stable?'

It was a clumsy lie and Lucy could see it had been a mistake to utter it. She clutched the bucket tighter, wondering if she dared use it as a weapon against any man who threatened Abigail or the children, or if resistance at this time would only make the consequences worse for all of them. They were, after all, heavily outnumbered.

At a word of command, the troops dismounted. They tethered their horses to the picket fence and fanned out across the yard in search of Robert. The sergeant swaggered up to the women and children, followed by two or three of his men.

'With your leave, ladies . . . '

'He's not in the house,' Abigail declared.

'If you don't mind, I'd rather be the

judge of that myself.'

Lucy darted a look at her sister-in-law. Was she telling the truth? It was hard to say. Abigail's face had taken on a closed expression. She and the sergeant exchanged hard stares, then she stepped across the threshold, ushering the older children ahead of her like a hen with her chicks.

'Are you looking for me?'

Robert's voice echoed across the yard. Every head turned. He was on the path from the house to the fields. Lucy guessed that the noises from the farmyard had carried on the still air and Robert had been attracted home by the possible threat to his family.

The sergeant nodded to two of his men. Clearly they had been given their orders prior to setting out on this mission because they made straight for Robert. Like Lucy before him, Robert changed his stance, stiffening as if about to resist and then checking the impulse as he assessed the odds.

57

'You Robert Prior?' the sergeant called.

Robert raised his chin higher. 'You know perfectly well I am, Abe Silcott.'

The two privates were now closing in on Robert, each on his own side. An unpleasant smile twisted Sergeant Silcott's lips and he groped in his coat pocket for a folded piece of parchment.

'Got a warrant for your arrest,' he said, conversationally.

'On what charge?'

'On the charge of harbouring damned British spies.'

Lucy felt as if the ground had been cut out from under her feet. So it was her fault after all. She had brought this trouble onto her family. She wanted to take the blame, but she knew that her confession would be seen as meaning that they were all guilty, even if she swore she was the only one who had known.

There was one advantage in having kept Selbourne's presence there a secret. Both Abigail and Robert uttered cries of unfeigned astonishment and nobody seemed to notice how silent Lucy had grown.

'And what proof do you have that this allegation is true?' Robert demanded.

Lucy noticed that he kept clenching and unclenching his fists, as if he was sorely tempted to knock down one or both of the guards that stood on either side of him. Then he glanced at Abigail and the children and Lucy knew her brother was not afraid of what the militiamen might do to him if he resisted, only afraid that those he loved most might witness a scene of violence.

'Oh, we've a very reliable witness that'll swear under oath to what he saw,' Sergeant Silcott replied. 'And I daresay we'll find more evidence soon enough.'

At a gesture from him, his men dispersed between the outbuildings and the farmhouse. Some headed straight for the hayloft, proving to Lucy beyond the shadow of a doubt who their witness must be. Crippled with guilt she dared not confess, she set down her bucket and took the white-faced Abigail in her arms, while the militiamen searched every corner of the farmstead.

Lucy was not sure what they expected to find. Did they really think Selbourne was still there? Or perhaps they did not expect to find anything at all and their mission was simply an excuse to smash and break and plunder the possessions of suspected Loyalists.

Abigail shuddered in Lucy's arms at the sound of breaking crockery, the splintering of furniture, the rip of a bayonet slicing through straw-filled mattresses. The two youngest children were crying by now. Only Jenny, looking pale and wide-eyed, clung silently to her mother's petticoats.

'Why are those bad men breaking up all our things?' she whispered.

'Because — because they think we did something wrong,' Lucy replied, but her voice shook. She had to stay calm, so as not to frighten the children any more than they were already.

'It'll all be over soon,' she added, hoping she was right. 'They'll go away again and we'll be able to clear things up and — ' She couldn't go on.

A man barged past them and spoke to the sergeant in a low tone. Other privates joined them from the various outbuildings, obviously reporting their findings, or lack of them, to their leader. There was now so much activity in the yard, Lucy hardly knew where to look. Sergeant Silcott was barking commands left and right.

'So did you find the evidence you were looking for?' Robert shouted.

Abigail shuddered again. Lucy knew Robert would be made to pay for this last act of defiance. The sergeant did not reply to him in words. Instead, he called to one of his men, who had saddled and bridled the Priors' one remaining plough horse.

'You can't take our horse. We need him here on the farm,' Lucy cried out, unable to restrain herself any longer.

And then she saw that the militiamen

were slinging sacks of grain across their saddles and loading up a cart they had brought with them with whatever provisions they could find. Others were rounding up all the livestock. A private passed close by the huddle of women and children, clutching their newly killed chickens by the legs.

Lucy cried out in protest, but in the din, nobody heard her. By now she was thoroughly frightened. Oh dear God, what have I done to my family? They took me in when I had nowhere else to go. Oh God, what can I do?

But worse was to come. Robert was ordered to mount his horse. Unable to bear inactivity a moment longer, Lucy broke away from the others.

'Where are you taking him?' she demanded.

'Didn't you hear? He's under arrest. And if he is found innocent, well, we could always do with another fine, strong, young fellow to join our ranks.'

'But we need him here. There's no other man on the farm. We won't be able to manage on our own.' Lucy wasn't sure it was wise to expose quite how vulnerable they were, but the words were out of her mouth before she could stop them.

The sergeant shrugged.

'That's none of my concern. I have my orders.'

Lucy bit back her next words. No, she would not beg him, though she could see that was clearly what the sergeant was hoping for.

There was one more shock awaiting her. Amid all the chaos, she suddenly became aware of the smell of smoke. Her head whipped round. Grey plumes were already rising from the barn. For the fire to be established so well, it must have been started several minutes previously, only in the confusion Lucy had failed to notice.

An involuntary cry broke from her lips.

'No! You can't do this. We have our children to feed. How will we live?'

The sergeant shrugged again and dug

his heels into the flanks of his horse.

'General Schuyler's orders.' He tossed the words over his shoulder. 'All food and forage that might otherwise fall into enemy hands must be destroyed.'

'But what about the children?'

'Do you really think any of us here cares what happens to Tory brats?'

With that he wheeled about and at the head of his motley band, he rode out of the gate. Robert almost disappeared in their midst, but he called above the din, 'Lucy, look after Abigail and the children!'

The cattle too were driven off. Both older children now were crying frantically for their father.

Losing her temper, Lucy shouted, 'Does it make you proud, to make war on women and children? Is this why you enlisted?'

As she looked from one face to another, she met stony stare after stony stare. Only a handful of the men glanced at her guiltily or avoided meeting her gaze and she knew they had qualms of conscience, but could not or would not go against the orders of their superiors because defending her would cost them dearly.

A cry from Abigail made Lucy turn around. Her heart sank. It was not only the barn that was on fire. It was the byre as well, with its precious store of hay, intended to last their stolen livestock the whole winter.

Abigail had already snatched up the bucket Lucy had abandoned earlier.

'Come on. We can't let this happen. Perhaps we can salvage something.'

Lucy was stirred into action. It was a relief to be doing something. They hauled bucket after bucket from the well and tried to beat out the flames with dampened sacks. With the loss of the livestock, the two women agreed that there was little point in wasting energy trying to save the byre. Instead they concentrated their efforts on the barn, leaving Jenny to mind the younger children since she was too young to help in any other way.

All too soon their muscles began to weep with the exertion. The heavy palls of smoke choked their lungs and made their eyes stream and the heat became so intense, it beat them back.

There was one vague hope in Lucy's heart that the sight of smoke might bring their neighbours to the rescue. With more people, they might at least be able to extinguish the fires, even if they were too late to save anything inside the burning buildings.

But time passed and nobody came. Perhaps their neighbours had enough work of their own to do, gathering what was left of the harvest. Or perhaps they had been warned off and dared not be seen helping the outlawed family, despite past friendships. That thought was even more bitter in Lucy's throat than the taste of smoke.

The log houses would have burnt only too well, even without such combustible materials as hay and straw and wheat inside. The fear grew in Lucy's heart that the fire might spread to engulf the farmhouse too, leaving them without a shelter during the bitter autumnal night. True, the ground was still damp after recent rain. But if this had happened in summer . . .

'It's no good, Lucy,' Abigail gasped, pulling her sister-in-law away after she had hurled one last bucketful of water at the barn with what little remained of her strength. 'The fire has taken too strong a hold. You need to rest before you collapse.'

Abigail herself looked as if she could barely keep on her feet any more.

'No! We can't let them defeat us this way,' Lucy protested, but her words came out as a wail of despair. She knew when she was beaten.

Abigail slumped on the ground, with her back against the wall of the farmhouse, and took the baby from Jenny's lap. Wearily she began unfastening the hooks on her bodice so she could suckle Caroline. Lucy found herself thinking that at least one of them would feed well that night. But she had been told that nursing mothers could lose their milk if they received a bad shock or were put under too much strain or deprived of food.

Lucy was drenched in sweat and her legs were quaking with exertion, but she dared not sit down, knowing that if she did, she would never be able to get up again. Instead she gathered the two older children to her side while she watched the black clouds of smoke and golden, leaping flames consume both outbuildings.

A whole year's worth of hard work, she thought. All gone in a matter of hours. Provisions for the winter and most of the spring looted or destroyed. She had no idea if anything edible still remained in the farmhouse.

The roof of the barn collapsed with a crash and both children hid their heads in Lucy's petticoats and covered their ears.

'Aunt Lucy, why did those bad men do this?' Jenny wailed.

How to explain all this destruction?

'Because — because — ' Because I tried to save a stranger? Because they don't agree with your father's politics? Because I refused to marry a man and he took his revenge on you as well as on me? Because this is what happens in war?

'Because — I don't know.'

The fire had almost burnt itself out in the byre. Perhaps it had been lit earlier, or maybe it was the straw and hay that had hastened the process. For a moment, Lucy saw an image of Selbourne curled up on his side, asleep in the hayloft. Now only charred ends of logs and heaps of grey ash remained. A few flames still danced along the surface, now leaping up, now wavering in the breeze, now sinking down into almost nothing.

The fire in the barn too was showing signs of abating. Perhaps they would be lucky. If the wind did not fan the flames, the fire might not spread any further. But how were they to live now, without cows to give milk or chickens to lay eggs? Without a horse left to pull the plough or the harrow? Without anyone strong enough to fell trees and rebuild the lost outbuildings?

'Aunt Lucy, what are we going to do now?'

Lucy swallowed, fighting off an insistent cough.

'We'll manage somehow,' she said. 'They can't beat us. Not this easily. We're Priors and we always fight back.'

5

The fighting words were small comfort to Lucy as the night began to close in, even if they seemed to console the children. She and Abigail managed to douse the last of the flames, thus safeguarding the house and the surrounding fields and forest. But the stench of burning still hovered over the yard.

It was with a good deal of trepidation that they ventured into the house to examine the damage and clear up as much of the mess as possible. Fortunately the raid had been carried out in haste and the destruction was not as wholesale as it might have been. Remembering the hangdog expressions of some of the men, Lucy even suspected some of them might have been deliberately half-hearted in their search for incriminating evidence.

There was little food left, but the Goodalls, an elderly Quaker couple who lived a few miles away, brought them some vegetables from the garden, a loaf of bread and a jug of milk for the children.

While Abigail scratched together a hasty meal, Lucy made some emergency repairs to the straw mattresses so they would have somewhere to sleep that night. But the sedentary task made her feel twitchy and restless. She kept wanting to go outside to feed the chickens or the pigs or milk the cows. The break in the routine left her disorientated and she found herself struggling to remember what other tasks needed to be done before bedtime.

In the presence of the children, both Lucy and Abigail strove to remain relentlessly cheerful, while fending off questions about when Papa would be coming home and reassuring them that the nasty men weren't going to come back. But it took longer than usual to settle the two older ones to sleep.

Only when all three children were asleep did the mask slip. Abigail sank onto one of the benches, rested her elbows on the table and put her head in her hands.

Lucy took a deep breath.

'Abigail,' she said.

'Yes?' Her sister-in-law raised her face. Lucy was startled to see how dry and hard her eyes looked, as if she would never be able to cry again.

Was this the right thing to do after all? With a twinge of foreboding, Lucy sat down near Abigail and stretched out her hand to squeeze her sister-in-law's fingers.

'I've — I've got a confession to make,' she blurted out, afraid that if she didn't say it now, she would never be able to say it at all. 'It's my fault all this happened. I'm really, really sorry and if I could do things differently . . . '

Her voice trailed away.

Abigail was gazing at her numbly. 'I don't understand. How could this be your fault?'

Lucy drew in another breath. Staring at the worn surface of the table because she couldn't look her sister-in-law in the eye, Lucy told her the whole story. At last she stuttered to a standstill, unnerved because she sensed that Abigail's eyes had never moved from her face.

'I'm really sorry, Abigail. I never thought things would end like this, or that Robert would be made to take the blame for my actions . . .'

Lucy darted a fleeting glance at her sister-in-law. Abigail uttered a deep sigh.

'You're both as bad as each other, you and Robert,' she said. 'It's my own fault for marrying into such a danger-ous family of firebrands.'

But her tone was resigned rather than angry. A glimmer of hope ignited in Lucy's heart.

'Does that mean — you'll forgive me?' she asked in a tiny voice.

Abigail sighed again and ran her hand through her hair, from brow to nape.

'Yes, I suppose so,' she said with the ghost of a smile. 'You did what you thought was right and can't be blamed that things went wrong.'

Impulsively Lucy jumped up and threw her arms around the other woman.

'Oh, you're the best sister I've ever had,' she declared.

'I'm the only sister you've ever had.'

'Yes, but that doesn't stop you being the best. And I swear, I'll do everything I can to set things right and help you provide for the children until — until Robert comes home.'

But the last words fell into a well of silence, echoing as they plunged down and downwards, because the same fear was lurking at the back of both of their minds. Suppose Robert never comes back at all.

* * *

Lucy passed a restless night, tormented by her thoughts. The only thing to be grateful for was that Abigail seemed to sleep soundly, worn out by her physical efforts and emotional strain.

By the time the first grey light of dawn appeared, Lucy could not bear inactivity any longer. She dressed herself quietly and crept downstairs and out into the yard.

The smell of charred wood still hung in the air. A few birds were chirruping in the forest, but otherwise everything was silent. No cockerel to crow at first light, no cows lowing, asking to have their burden of milk lightened, not a bleat or a grunt or a human footstep save her own.

The yard was lightly dusted with frost. Lucy crunched across it to inspect the damage. She thought she could still feel a faint warmth emanating from the blackened ruins, though perhaps that was only her imagination.

The chill of the morning was a reminder that winter was not far off and Lucy shivered, wondering how they would manage for food. They had not much money and not much left of value to sell. Besides, she wasn't sure how many people would be willing to trade with them, now they had been singled out as the enemy.

She had half-hoped to find that the destruction was not as bad as she remembered, that perhaps something could be salvaged, that something had been miraculously saved from the fire. But as she tentatively poked one charred log with the toe of her shoe, it splintered into smaller fragments. The only thing it was fit for was to be burnt on the hearth in the farmhouse.

Her eyes smarted. Her head throbbed from lack of sleep and every muscle in her body ached. Her throat was still dry and itchy and she dreaded the possibility of another gut-wrenching coughing fit. The whole world seemed still and grey, dark shapes just emerging from a faint autumnal mist.

Something scuffed the ground behind her. Lucy whirled round, alert to possible danger, her hands clenching into fists. She gasped. There was a dark figure, roughly the size and shape of a man, standing beside the farmhouse, apparently watching her.

She drew back, intending to snatch up a charred log end as a weapon. The figure took two steps towards her.

'Miss Prior,' a deep voice whispered. 'Tell me what happened here. I never thought . . . '

In the dim morning light, away from the shadow of the farmhouse, Lucy recognised the man. It was Joseph Selbourne.

'They came looking for you yesterday,' she replied in a cold, hard tone. 'And when they couldn't find you, they took away my brother and all the livestock and our winter stores . . . '

The fury was rising inexorably inside her.

'Oh God, I'm sorry. I never imagined . . . '

' . . . and it's all your fault,' she cut across his words ruthlessly.

Suddenly she had launched herself at

him, drumming at his breast with both fists, hardly aware that a pair of strong arms had wrapped lightly around her waist and back.

'I hate you. I hate you. I wish you'd never come,' she sobbed.

'Ssh, Lucy, I'm so sorry.'

Without meaning to, she uttered a loud, hiccuping sob. A large hand moulded itself against the back of her head and pressed her face against a broad shoulder.

She was crying uncontrollably now with all the pent-up emotions from the previous day. Only gradually she became aware of the strong, warm arms wrapped tight around her. Selbourne was gently rubbing her shoulder blade and murmuring soft words, not urging her to stop crying, but apologising over and over again.

At length Lucy's sobs subsided, leaving her exhausted and shivery. She rubbed the heel of one hand against her eyes. Selbourne was still pressing her tight against his breast. She could hear the echo of his heart and she was aware that her tears had soaked right through his shirt. And yet it was incredibly tempting to stay there, safely cocooned in this stranger's arms, and rely on him for the support she felt she needed so badly.

'I'm sorry for giving way like that,' she mumbled, trying reluctantly to prise herself away.

'Don't be sorry. You needed a good cry.'

'I shouldn't have hit you or said I hated you.' She cringed at her behaviour.

'It doesn't matter. You were upset.'

Nonetheless, Lucy was embarrassed. She straightened up and Selbourne loosened his grip. His hands slid down her arms so he could clasp both her hands.

'What are you doing back here?' she asked.

He hesitated, then glanced up at the lightening sky. 'Maybe it would be better if we took shelter somewhere before I tell you any more.'

Instantly Lucy stiffened. 'Why? Do you think there is anything more they can do to us than they've already done, if we're caught?'

Selbourne ducked his head, but did not reply to her reproach. Lucy bit her lip, realising what he had meant. Apart from the roof over their heads, there was nothing more she and her family could lose. But Selbourne stood to lose his life if he was caught by his enemies.

He released her hands and, bereft of the warmth of his body, Lucy shivered.

'I'm sorry,' she said. 'I didn't mean — you'd best come inside.'

She led the way, but was brought up short on the threshold. Abigail was sitting in the most comfortable chair in the kitchen, with Caroline in her arms. Robert had had that chair made while Abigail was pregnant with their first child, to make it easier for her to nurse her baby.

Abigail's head whisked round at the sound of the door and instinctively she tugged at her open bodice at the sight of the stranger standing behind Lucy.

'I'm sorry, Abigail. I didn't know you were up . . . ' Lucy stammered.

'Please forgive this intrusion,' Selbourne said, removing his hat, 'though that's the least of my offences. My name is Joseph Selbourne.'

Lucy saw a shadow flit across Abigail's face. The latter swallowed hard before she could bring herself to reply.

'Lucy told me about you last night,' she replied in studiedly neutral tones.

Lucy had absolutely no idea whether she was likely to let loose one of her rare bursts of anger, or if she would take this development in her stride as she did almost everything else.

Slowly Abigail rose to her feet, the baby clutched to her like a shield.

'I cannot apologise enough for bringing such disaster upon your family,' Selbourne went on.

'Why are you here?'

It was only because she knew Abigail

so well that Lucy could detect the barely contained anger in her voice.

Selbourne drew in a deep breath.

'A number of reasons. For one thing, I had a presentiment of evil before I left this place and I wanted to make sure you were all safe.' He smiled wryly.

'But your mission,' Lucy protested. Surely he could be court-martialled for failing to carry out his duties?

Selbourne hesitated for a long moment.

'I couldn't get through,' he said at last, barely audibly. 'Burgoyne's Northern Army is entirely surrounded and he is suing for peace.'

Shock registered in the faces of both women. They had heard rumours that things were not going well for Burgoyne and his mixed British, Brunswicker and Canadian troops, but it was difficult to know what to believe when each side distorted the news according to their own purposes.

'So what will you do now?' Lucy asked.

'The only thing I can do — return to

Fort Clinton and resume my duties.'

'Fort Clinton? But isn't that — ?'

'We took both Fort Clinton and Fort Montgomery by storm from the Americans on October 6th. My mission, had I been able to carry it out, was to offer Burgoyne reinforcements from the south.'

Lucy was aware that he was revealing highly sensitive information in an effort to gain their trust. It was agonising to think how close rescue had come for Burgoyne and his men. If Selbourne could have reached them a day or two sooner . . .

There was a long silence in the room, interrupted only by a grizzled protest from the baby. Abigail propped Caroline against her shoulder and began rubbing and patting her back to ease her trapped wind.

'Why are you telling us all this? Aren't you afraid we might betray you in order to try to exchange you for my husband?' Abigail asked.

'I wouldn't blame you if you did

exactly that,' Selbourne said. 'I do, however, have another proposal.' He leaned both hands on the table and looked from one woman to the other.

'Well?' Abigail asked, mistrustfully.

'I want you to come with me,' he said quietly. 'If I had more time, I'd help you to rebuild the destroyed outbuildings. But that won't help you to survive the winter here without adequate supplies. What I can offer you is my protection on the journey . . . '

'You want us to take three young children on foot to a fort hundreds of miles away?' Abigail asked, as if she thought he was mad.

'I'm sure transport could be procured along the way to take you to New York or some other place of safety. Once Burgoyne has surrendered in form, do you think you will be safe here from further reprisals?'

'But what about my husband? What if he comes back and finds us gone? What if — '

'Mrs Prior, I think you know as well

as I do how unlikely that is under the present circumstances,' Selbourne said gently, but Abigail ducked her head and blinked back a tear. 'When I get back to headquarters, I'll use what influence I have to get some information about your husband. And perhaps between the three of us, we can devise some way of letting him know where you are going without putting you in any danger if the message should miscarry.'

Abigail looked around at the room, taking in every little object. Lucy knew exactly what she was thinking and feeling. Abandoning her home and husband for the sake of her children would have been hard enough in normal circumstances. But they all knew that the journey would not be without its hazards, particularly with three young children in tow. If Selbourne was intercepted and unmasked as a British officer in civilian dress, he could still be hanged as a spy. Without him as a protector, they might be left stranded in hostile territory, with even less than they possessed now.

'I don't want to hurry you into a decision,' Selbourne said after a pause, 'but time is pressing. Sooner or later, I will have to go, with you or without you, if I do not want to be shot as a deserter. I'd like to be able to make at least partial amends for having brought this trouble on your family.'

The silence that followed Selbourne's last words was suddenly broken by a scuffle from the stairs. They turned just in time to see two little, white-clad figures come tumbling into the room, crying, 'Papa!'

Then the children's steps faltered as they looked up at Selbourne's face. One plump little fist shot up to Robin's mouth and he sidled over to Lucy, who was the nearest of the two women. Jenny meanwhile stood her ground, nightgown or not.

She fixed Selbourne with a stern look and said accusingly, 'You're not Papa.'

'No, I'm afraid not,' Selbourne replied, crouching to bring his face to the same level as hers. 'But I've come to see if I can help your mamma and auntie while Papa is away.'

Jenny seemed fairly satisfied with this explanation, though she glanced at her mother and aunt for confirmation.

'When is Papa coming home?'

All three adults exchanged looks.

'We don't know, sweetheart,' Selbourne replied. 'But he loves you and your brother and sister' — the last word came out as a question and Lucy nodded silently — 'very much and if he can find a way of getting back to you, I'm sure he will.'

'Come along you two,' Abigail interrupted, obviously finding the conversation about Robert too painful. 'It's high time you were washed and dr- oh my God.'

Her eyes had inadvertently turned towards the window and the colour drained from the face.

'What is it?' Lucy demanded, whirling towards the window. But before she could catch sight of what had alarmed

Abigail, the latter was sweeping them all towards the stairs.

'Get that man and the children out of sight,' Abigail hissed. 'It's Isaac Wilcox.'

6

She wanted to protest that the children were in no danger from Isaac Wilcox, but then Lucy realised that they might inadvertently betray Selbourne, which would only make matters worse for everyone.

'You get Mr Selbourne out of sight — I'll go and talk to Mr Wilcox,' she said.

'Are you sure?' Abigail asked.

Lucy shrugged, trying to feign a nonchalance she did not feel. He was the last person she wanted to see after the events of the previous day.

'It's me he's come to see, or so I imagine,' she said dryly.

Without glancing back at the others for fear of losing her nerve, Lucy went out into the yard. She closed the door firmly behind her and planted herself in front of it so Wilcox could not enter without pushing her aside.

'Come to gloat over your handiwork?' she called across the yard.

Wilcox looked somewhat shamefaced at the sight of the burnt-out ruins. Then Lucy saw him draw together all his reserves of dignity and self-confidence.

'What makes you think this has anything to do with me?'

'I thought your threats against my family, and me in particular, were explicit enough.'

Wilcox shifted uneasily.

'Those weren't threats,' he mumbled, 'just friendly warnings. I'd hate to see anything bad happen to your family, Miss Prior, and that's a fact.'

Maybe he was sincere, at least to a degree, but it didn't stop Lucy from suspecting his motives.

'Well, something bad has happened. I'm surprised you dare show your face around here after all your warnings.'

He spread his hands in an effort to deflect her anger. Lucy could feel herself trembling. She was not sure how long her anger would sustain her, particularly if she provoked Wilcox too far and he became aggressive.

'I came to see if I could help out — you know the offer of marriage is still open. I'll even take in your sister and her children, give them a roof over their heads for the winter . . . '

'How very generous of you,' Lucy drawled. 'However, we do still have a roof, even if we have precious little else left.'

'But that is precisely why you ought to consider my offer. I'll take care of you all. I'll even see what I can do about your brother.'

For a moment Lucy wavered. Was she being selfish in rejecting Wilcox's offer? For Robert's sake and Abigail's and, most of all, for the children, should she perhaps consider marrying Isaac Wilcox? After all, she was the one responsible for their present predicament.

If she said yes, they could all stay in the neighbourhood. Robert would have no difficulty finding them, if he was released at some point in the future. But oh, could she bear to be chained to Isaac Wilcox for the remainder of her life? Was it too high a price to pay?

'You know how comfortable things are at my place,' Wilcox went on. 'Prime piece of land, better than this one, as far as I can make out, and closer to town as well . . .'

Lucy jumped as the door sprang open behind her.

'Thank you kindly for your generous offer, Mr Wilcox, but I wouldn't dream of letting Lucy sell herself for the sake of my family,' Abigail interrupted firmly.

'Oh, but . . .' Lucy stopped herself. If she admitted in front of Isaac Wilcox that this situation was all her fault, there was no saying what the consequences might be.

'We've always managed well enough in the past and we'll manage in the future too,' Abigail said, cutting short Wilcox's protests about their friendless, foodless condition.

He decided to change tack.

'It's your choice, Miss Prior,' he said, pointedly ignoring Abigail. 'You going to let your family starve for the sake of pride and anger?'

'Lucy!' Abigail said in a warning tone as her sister-in-law took a step forward.

'Don't worry, Abigail. I won't let you or the children starve. And I won't let myself be blackmailed either,' she added, turning from Abigail towards Wilcox. 'Thank you for your offer, sir, but we'll manage as we are.'

Wilcox shrugged, but Lucy could see from his scowl that he did not feel as nonchalant as he was pretending. 'It's your loss,' he said. 'Good day to you both. I wish you luck in all your undertakings.'

He could not prevent a sneer from creeping into his voice, as if he thought the women might be reduced to begging him for help, once winter set in and all their other resources ran out. Lucy wouldn't even have put it past him to reject their pleas if they left it too long, to revenge himself for this slight.

But he doesn't know us if he thinks we'll beg him, or anyone else, Lucy thought, digging her nails deep into her palms.

They watched Isaac Wilcox's departure in silence. Then Lucy turned to her sister-in-law.

'So, Abigail,' she said slowly, 'what are we going to do now?'

Abigail shrugged and again Lucy was not deceived by a show of casualness.

'The only thing we can do,' Abigail replied. 'We'll have to accept Selbourne's offer to escort us all or part of the way to New York.'

★ ★ ★

Once the decision had been made, it was remarkable how quickly their preparations could be completed. With help from Selbourne, Lucy and Abigail packed what little remained of the food, some essential clothes for the children and everything of value that could be carried easily, so they had something to sell or pawn when their money ran out.

Selbourne's advice was invaluable. As a soldier, he was used to living in all manner of conditions and he knew what might prove useful if they were forced to shelter in the forest overnight or cook over a bonfire.

At Selbourne's suggestion, Abigail wrote a letter to Robert, explaining that they had gone to New York. Once the letter was sealed, Lucy took it to the Goodalls' farm. As Quakers, they had no reason to love the new regime and they had proved their kindness by their actions of the previous night. Lucy told Mrs Goodall that she and Abigail were leaving with the children, though she made no reference to Selbourne.

'If Robert comes looking for us, you will give him the letter, won't you?'

'Indeed I will. But hast thou thought carefully about taking this step?' Mrs Goodall asked, gazing earnestly in her face. 'Tis a long and arduous road ahead of thee and thine.'

Lucy was tempted to tell her about Selbourne — surely she was trustworthy enough? But at the last minute she decided against it.

'I know, but we can hardly stay here without any means of keeping body and soul together. In a city, we might be able to find work sewing or washing.'

Mrs Goodall tutted but made no further attempt to convince her to stay.

'Well, I'll remember you in my prayers tonight,' she said. 'But let me give thee a bit of food for the journey.'

Lucy made only a token protest. The Goodalls were not overly wealthy, but Lucy didn't want to offend them by spurning their help. Nor could she refuse the generous offer for the sake of the children. She did, however, persuade Mrs Goodall to accept a small sum out of the money Selbourne had given her for his board and lodgings.

Mrs Goodall's last hug and kiss brought tears to Lucy's eyes, knowing as she did that it was unlikely she would ever see her kindly neighbour again.

As she returned to her brother's farm, she was acutely aware that this was the last time she would see these familiar scenes. The sight of the farmyard with its burnt-out ruins gave her another pang. Without any farm animals or the children playing in the yard, the place looked abandoned already.

Inside it was quite another story. Abigail and Selbourne were still making last minute preparations. The two older children, caught between excitement and anxiety about the future, kept asking questions and getting under the feet of the adults.

Jenny tugged Lucy by the petticoats and asked, 'Are we going to find Papa?'

Lucy hesitated. The look of hope in the little girl's eyes was heartbreaking, but she knew it would be wrong to raise false hopes.

'No, but we're going somewhere safe and when Papa — has finished what he's doing now, he'll come and find us,' she said, sending up a silent prayer that her words might come true. 'I've left a letter with Mrs Goodall, to tell Papa where we've gone so he'll be able to follow us.'

Abigail too was striving to remain cheerful, though Lucy could see what a wrench it was for her to leave. This had been her home far longer than it had been Lucy's. All three of her children had been born in the big wooden bed upstairs and nursed in the comfortable chair by the hearth.

At last they were ready to go. It was a risk, leaving in broad daylight, particularly for Selbourne, but it couldn't be helped.

'We can hardly take the children through dense forest at night, unless we had some sort of cart or carriage,' Selbourne said with a shake of his head, 'and the more ground we can cover before nightfall, the better.'

The adults picked up their bundles or knapsacks. Abigail lifted Caroline out of her cradle for the last time. The baby had been asleep after a hearty meal and she uttered a sleepy protest before settling down on her mother's breast, smacking her lips as she did so. Lucy took charge of Robin while Jenny, always the most daring of the children, agreed to hold hands with 'Uncle Joseph', as she was already calling Selbourne.

'It's better that the children think of me as a member of the family,' Selbourne had explained to the two young women. 'They are less likely to betray me accidentally that way.' He added after a moment's thought, 'Perhaps you ought to call me Joseph too.'

It seemed an unprecedented familiarity to Lucy to address a virtual stranger by his first name, but she could see why it was necessary, to protect his identity and make sure they were not deprived of their protector. By the same token, of course, Selbourne — Joseph — would have to call them Lucy and Abigail, and somehow the thought made her shiver.

Lucy glanced back at the farm one last time as they reached the edge of the forest. Then she compressed her lips, squeezed Robin's hand encouragingly and lifted her chin as she followed the others into the shade of the forest.

For the first part of the journey, they kept to the least frequented roads Abigail and Lucy knew, anxious not to meet any of their neighbours. What Lucy feared most was that they might encounter Isaac Wilcox or one of his friends. If he knew she was leaving, she was irrationally afraid he might try to stop them, by one means or another.

They had to go at a steady speed. Jenny and Robin's legs were short and, as Selbourne said, they had to pace themselves carefully so as not to exhaust themselves too soon. Robin, inevitably, was the first to flag and start suggesting to his aunt that she ought to carry him and that he had had enough of walking and wanted to go home.

'I'll tell you what,' Selbourne said,

suddenly crouching down beside the boy, 'how would you like to ride on my shoulders?'

Abashed, Robin dropped his eyelashes and tried to hide behind Lucy's petticoats.

'It'll be just like riding a horse,' Selbourne said, 'and you'll be able to see much further ahead than anyone else because you'll be even taller than me.'

Jenny clapped her hands together in excitement.

'What about me? Can I ride on your shoulders?' she begged.

Selbourne hesitated and Lucy intervened.

'I think you might be too heavy for Mr — Uncle Joseph,' she corrected herself just in time.

Jenny pouted. 'I'm not very big yet,' she said, 'and I'm ever so tired too, more tireder than Robin is.'

'No, you're not. I'm tireder 'n you,' Robin insisted.

'Hush, the pair of you,' Abigail

intervened. She was jogging the baby wearily to try to still the preliminary croaks that might well become full-blown wails soon. 'You're upsetting your sister. What will Uncle Joseph think of you if you squabble like that?'

Neither child seemed satisfied with this and both glowered at each other, even though they didn't say anything more. It was not often that Abigail used that tone with them and that alone told Lucy how worried her sister-in-law was.

'I'll tell you what,' Selbourne said hastily, 'if Robin wants to, I'll carry him first, because he's the littlest, and when he has rested, then it will be your turn, Jenny.'

'Robin isn't the littlest; Caroline is,' Jenny pointed out.

'Ah, but she's too little to ride on my shoulders.'

'Won't you exhaust yourself?' Lucy objected.

Selbourne smiled and unexpectedly, dizzyingly, her heart gave a leap.

'Don't worry about me,' he said. 'I

wouldn't offer if I didn't think I could do it.'

Having seen how much Jenny wanted to ride on Uncle Joseph's shoulders was enough to change Robin's mind about its desirability. Lucy lifted him into position and then picked up her bundle again.

Robin looked a little alarmed when Selbourne drew himself up to his full height, but once he had got used to it, the boy seemed to enjoy his new elevation. He even kicked his heels against Selbourne's breast as he had seen his father do to urge on his horse. The only possible danger was from low, sweeping branches, but Selbourne was careful how he picked his way along.

Lucy held out her hand to Jenny, who had been watching her new found uncle and brother with her lower lip stuck out in a pout.

'I hate being the oldest,' she muttered. Instead of taking her aunt's hand, she kicked a pebble on the path.

'No, you don't. You know you like

being stronger than Robin and able to walk much further than him. Besides which,' Lucy dropped her voice to a mysterious whisper, 'if you were riding on Uncle Joseph's shoulders, I couldn't tell you any secrets.'

'What sort of secrets?' Jenny asked, half-mollified.

'Come here and I'll tell you.'

★ ★ ★

Joseph Selbourne was as good as his word. Once Jenny's steps began to drag painfully, he crouched down so Lucy could lift a reluctant Robin off his shoulders and help Jenny scramble up in her brother's place.

'Are you sure she's not too heavy?' Abigail and Lucy chorused, as if they had rehearsed their lines.

Selbourne smiled.

'I've carried heavier weights than this,' he said. 'You do realise you should both make a wish? At least, where I come from, there's a superstition that if two people say the same thing at the same moment, they can each have a wish granted, as long as they don't tell anyone what it is.'

'Where do you come from?' Lucy asked, after hastily wishing that they would all reach their journey's end safe and well and be reunited with Robert, and then wondering if that counted as two wishes instead of one.

'Nottinghamshire. What about you? Were you born in America, or did you emigrate from somewhere else?'

'Abigail is from Boston, but Robert and I were born in Lincolnshire. Our parents came to America to seek a better life when we were about the same age as Robin and Jenny are now.'

Something in Lucy's tone made Joseph glance at her out of the corner of his eye.

'Your parents are both dead, aren't they?' he asked gently.

'Yes. That's why Robert asked me to come and help him and Abigail on the farm.'

Selbourne didn't probe any deeper, something Lucy was relieved about. She wasn't very far from tears, but she knew she mustn't cry in front of the children. There were still times when she missed her parents badly. She knew if they had still been alive, she and Abigail could have gone to stay with them in this present crisis.

Towards evening, Selbourne built a shelter in the forest for them, with the others helping where they could. Even Robin and Jenny collected broken twigs for the fire, though they had strict instructions not to go out of sight of the adults. Their earlier differences forgotten, the two children even managed to drag a broken bough, longer than the two of them put together, to the bivouac and looked suitably proud when all three adults praised them for their efforts.

They shared their supper by the fireside, before Abigail made the children wash in a nearby stream and then shooed them into the tiny improvised hut. Lucy was left alone with Selbourne for the first time since she had discovered him in the yard. Logically speaking, she knew that had only happened that morning, but it felt longer ago.

'You're very good with the children,' Lucy remarked, trying to obliterate the image in her head of her hurling herself at Selbourne in a fury and him catching her in his arms.

'Thank you.'

'Do you — have you — do you have any children of your own?'

She tried to pretend she had not been planning to ask that question ever since he had volunteered to carry the children, but her face was glowing. She could only hope he would think she was fire-flushed from the bonfire near which they were still sitting.

'No. I'm not married.'

He uttered the words simply, but Lucy recognised a weight of sadness behind them. In the circumstances, she felt it would have been flippant to point out that, as a gentleman, it was not impossible for him to have had children without being married.

'My childhood sweetheart promised to wait for me and then married someone else while I was posted to Ireland.'

'Oh, I'm so sorry.'

'Don't be. We were both young and foolish at the time and neither of us knew then how hard life can be for a soldier's wife, especially in times of war.'

Lucy gazed at his handsome face against the brightness of the fire and wondered if she dared ask him any more. But before she could formulate a question, Abigail crept out to join them for a whispered discussion about their plans for the morrow.

7

Lucy passed an uncomfortable night in the shack Selbourne had constructed. Despite the pile of dry leaves and undergrowth they had collected to serve as mattresses, she could feel the hard, cold earth beneath. Whenever someone stirred, the bedding rustled, making Lucy start, convinced she had heard the stealthy footstep of a wolf or bear, prowling around outside.

They lay closely packed together, save for Selbourne, who slept a little apart, nearer to the doorway. They were all fully clothed beneath the cloaks and blankets they had brought with them, but even so it was a cold night. The children found it difficult to settle in such an alien environment and Caroline woke at least twice, demanding to be fed or complaining about her sore gums.

Most of all Lucy worried about Selbourne's presence. If it had been Robert curled up by the entrance, a loaded pistol close at hand in case of emergency, she would have been able to rest more easily.

But Selbourne was a stranger. He had done nothing to make her think he was anything but a gentleman or that he meant to harm her or her family. And yet she could not help feeling unsettled. She, after all, was responsible for her family's plight, by sheltering Selbourne and rejecting Wilcox's offer of protection, thus ultimately driving them to make this long and potentially hazardous journey.

When she woke from her unrefreshing drowse the following morning, her limbs ached from sleeping on the hard ground. Abigail and Selbourne were already up. Leaving the children to sleep, Lucy scrambled outside to join the others, who were building a bonfire, so Abigail could warm some water to bathe Caroline before they set out.

'Good morning, Sleeping Beauty,' Selbourne greeted her. 'Did you sleep well?'

'No, not particularly.' She added hastily, 'I daresay I'll get used to living like this pretty quickly.'

'I hope there will be no need for that. I'll endeavour to provide more comfortable lodgings in the future.'

Silence descended over the clearing in the forest after Abigail retreated into the bivouac to change the baby's napkin. While Lucy searched their packs for some breakfast, Selbourne produced a miniature shaving kit from his coat pocket. He set about lathering his jawline and then drawing his cut-throat razor in long, smooth strokes along his skin. Lucy watched him out of the corner of her eye, somehow relishing the intimacy of the scene.

It was only when Selbourne glanced up at her, as if sensing her gaze, that she remembered her own dishevelled appearance.

'I must look a sight,' she said,

beginning to take the pins out of her hair so she could comb it through and fasten it back in a knot at the top of her head.

'You look remarkably pretty to me.'

Selbourne's words startled her into glancing at his face and she blushed when she discovered he was gazing at her with a slight smile quirking his lips.

'You're flattering me, Mr Selbourne,' she said.

'Indeed I am not. And I thought we agreed that you would call me Joseph.'

His fingertips touched her hair and Lucy's heart leapt into her throat. She found herself unable to move or tear her gaze away, suddenly convinced that he was going to kiss her.

Then he withdrew his hand and she realised with a pang of disappointment and shame that he had merely been picking a dead leaf out of her hair. She blushed even more fiercely, afraid he might have guessed what was passing through her mind. Of course Joseph Selbourne wouldn't take advantage of her in that way. He was too much of a gentleman and she was a silly, over-imaginative farm girl.

She turned abruptly away from him, relieved at hearing the children's voices inside the bivouac.

'I'd better go and help Abigail,' she said and failed to notice that Joseph watched her retreat with a wistful look in his eyes.

If Lucy thought the first day was hard enough, she was soon to discover that things were not going to get any easier the further they went. Her feet became blistered from the miles they walked. Her arms and shoulders ached from carrying her pack and, increasingly often, one of the children too. Their food ran out, which lightened their loads slightly, but meant they were forced to stop in towns or villages, even at isolated farms, to try to buy or barter for fresh supplies.

Lucy learned far more about human nature than she had ever wanted to know during these forays. She was surprised how often apparently wealthy people sent them away empty-handed, even if the children were crying from tiredness or hunger, while people not much better off than themselves freely shared their stores or offered them a place to stay the night, and then sometimes didn't even want to accept payment.

Wherever possible, Joseph tried to find a barn or a small country inn to shelter them for the night. But there was never enough time to wash and dry Caroline's napkins properly. In the end, Lucy sacrificed one of her petticoats, tearing it into rough squares so her youngest niece could be kept reasonably clean and dry.

On top of everything else, Lucy often found herself worrying about her brother. Was Robert even alive? She couldn't speak about such things in Abigail's hearing or the children's and opportunities to talk to Joseph alone were limited.

Their route southwards never strayed

too far from the banks of the Hudson, though they were forced to detour now and then to avoid swamps or find bridges or fords across tributaries that flowed into the larger river. Joseph had a map and a compass and though she did not dare ask him, Lucy formed the impression that at least part of their route was familiar to him from earlier missions, carrying messages or scouting out the terrain.

Lucy saw him stiffen whenever they encountered Continental regulars or militia. But amazingly, the children seemed to act as the perfect camouflage. No one expected a British officer on a secret mission to be travelling with such an entourage.

The weather deteriorated as autumn set in in good earnest. The children caught colds from being exposed to rain and wind. All three had grown grumpy as the days passed. Sometimes Robin and Jenny were so tired, they no longer wanted to play when they stopped for a rest. But at least they had accepted

Joseph as a member of the family. After his initial mistrust, Robin had come to hero-worship Uncle Joseph almost as much as Jenny did. The girl even confided to Lucy in a hot little whisper that she thought Uncle Joseph was very handsome, like a prince in a fairy story.

The two women had been warier, particularly Abigail. But Joseph was such a perfect gentleman, their reserve melted like snow in the spring sunshine. Within a matter of days, Lucy felt as if she had known him the whole of her life.

He revealed nothing about his military career, not even his rank or his regiment. Instead he talked about growing up on the edge of what remained of Sherwood Forest.

'Although until I came to America, I had no idea forests could be so vast and impenetrable,' he admitted with a rueful laugh.

He amused the children with tales about the mischief he and his brothers had got up to, sliding down the banisters, clambering into a horse chestnut tree near the garden gates to throw snowballs at passing carriages, or frightening each other by telling ghost stories after they were meant to be asleep.

'The only trouble was that Harry, my youngest brother, had nightmares as a result and he blurted out the truth to our mother. She made us promise to stop and of course we couldn't go back on a promise, not to our mother, no matter how tempting it was.'

Abigail shook her head, but she was smiling.

'I hope you don't give my older two any ideas,' she said. 'We have quite enough trouble as it is.'

Joseph was about to reply, but suddenly he raised his head as if his ear had caught some unexpected noise. Lucy too braced herself and shushed Jenny, who had started to ask a question. Now she could hear it too — the unmistakeable thud of hooves. And not just one horse either. Few, if any, farmers had more than one horse any more; they were in such demand by the armies and militias on both sides, not only to mount the cavalry, but to pull supply wagons and field guns. The sound could only mean one thing.

Joseph looked around for some cover, but it was already too late. A troop of horsemen had just rounded a bend in the road. All the pedestrians could do was usher the older children to the side of the track to prevent them from being mown down.

Lucy could tell from the set of Joseph's shoulders that he was expecting trouble. He was not mistaken. At a word from their leader, the cavalrymen drew to a halt beside the huddle of civilians.

'Are you from these parts?'

'No, sir,' Joseph replied, 'I'm afraid not.'

They had agreed amongst themselves not to volunteer any information about themselves unless they were asked directly. That way they stood a better chance of not contradicting themselves and so being caught out in a lie.

The officer narrowed his eyes, as if he did not quite believe Joseph. Perhaps he thought Joseph was lying in order to avoid acting as a guide to them. Or maybe Joseph's tone had not been deferential enough, though he was scrupulously polite.

'Where are you from then?'

'Up north,' Joseph replied, 'not far from Saratoga.'

Still the officer didn't look convinced.

'You're a long way from home,' he said, glancing at the children.

Lucy couldn't help being aware of the way some of the men were leering at her and Abigail from their vantage point on horseback. One man would not be enough to protect them if they decided to do anything untoward.

'We didn't have much choice,' she intervened. 'Everything we had was confiscated or burned to prevent it from falling into enemy hands.'

She used her sweetest, most winsome tone, to try to hide any trace of bitterness in her voice. The officer grunted.

'Where are you heading?'

'To stay with relatives near Esopus, at least until something else can be arranged,' Joseph replied, throwing Lucy a warning glance.

The officer uttered a cynical laugh and his horse danced beneath him. He brought the creature under control with a firm hand.

'Well, good luck to you,' he said with heavy irony. And then at a word of command, the whole troop moved on again.

Joseph frowned as he turned to watch them go.

'I don't like the sound of that,' he said. 'He knew something he didn't tell us.'

Lucy had come to the same conclusion herself and she glanced at Abigail.

'Well, what should we do?' Abigail

asked, patting Caroline's back absent-mindedly.

'Proceed cautiously, I suppose,' Joseph said, 'and hope we meet some friendlier informant along the way.'

It was not till evening that they finally got the information they sought. By then the children had begun to drag their feet and Lucy found herself tripping over tangled tree roots in her tiredness. The soles of her feet felt raw, but she dared not complain, because she knew she had to set a good example. She couldn't imagine how she would be able to get up tomorrow, let alone continue the journey.

Conversation had sunk almost to nothing. No one had the energy for the jokes, stories or songs they had traded in the morning when they were still fresh. The sun had sunk and only a livid streak illuminated the horizon by the time they reached one of the small towns that were scattered along the Hudson and its tributaries. In all the time since they encountered the patrol, they had hardly seen a soul, except from a vast distance.

The town was not large and it was easy enough to find what appeared to be the only inn in the place. Perhaps that was also why it was so over-crowded. As soon as Joseph opened the door, they were assailed by the heat, noise and stench of the place. Wood smoke, tobacco, boiled cabbage, sweat and beer fumes thickened the air. The taproom teemed with human bodies, so the barmaids and waiters were hard-pressed to find their way between the tables and benches. The light was dim, except around the blazing fire, and the air blue with smoke, obscuring the faces of those within.

In normal circumstances, neither Abigail nor Lucy would have set foot in such a rough place. Joseph elbowed his way towards the bar, a sleepy Jenny astride his hip, her head tucked against his shoulder. Lucy and Abigail followed with the younger children.

Looking around, Lucy was struck by

how many other women and children were there, from a tiny, mewling infant, even younger than Caroline, to a pair of toothless crones, sitting in a corner, huddled and shapeless under the blankets they had wrapped round their shoulders, despite the closeness of the room.

'It must be market day, or something like that,' Abigail murmured.

With some difficulty, Joseph had located the landlord amid the throng.

' . . . any room no matter how small . . . ' Lucy just caught the last of his words above the din.

The landlord looked Joseph up and down, a shrewd look in his eyes.

'Let's see the colour of your money first,' he said. 'I've no room for vagabonds and charity cases.'

Joseph flushed at the implied insult, but Lucy placed a restraining hand on his arm. She could feel how tense his muscles were.

'How much are you asking?'

The sum the landlord named seemed

extortionate, particularly when they saw how tiny the room was that he had allotted to them. It contained a bedstead, a washstand, a deal table, a plain chair and nothing more.

'You've nothing better?' Joseph asked.

The landlord shrugged. 'That's all that's left.'

'You do seem rather busy,' Lucy remarked, allowing Abigail to squeeze into the room first to deposit Robin on the bed. 'Is something particular happening here tonight?'

The landlord looked at her in surprise.

'Not as far as I know,' he said with a hard laugh. 'I'd have thought you'd know better than me what's brought all these folks hither.'

Lucy glanced at Joseph and Abigail, but they both looked as baffled as she felt.

'I'm sorry. I don't understand.'

'You're not from Esopus, then?'

'No.'

Esopus was a town some miles

further south, not far from the Hudson and located on one of its tributaries. There had been some talk that they might venture that way, though their plans were still unsettled.

'What's happened at Esopus?' Joseph asked.

He had placed Jenny on the bed beside her brother and Abigail sat down on its edge as if she was afraid her legs wouldn't bear her weight any longer.

'Been burnt down by the British Army,' the landlord said, 'on account some fools fired a few cannon at their ships but didn't wait long enough for them to be within range.'

All Joseph's tiredness seemed to have dropped away from him, Lucy thought as she glanced at his animated face. He looked like a hound before the start of a hunt.

'Where are the British ships now?' he asked.

'As far as I know, they're still out there,' the landlord replied with a sniff. 'Can't say how many miles downriver.

They do say they're wending this way, though Putnam'll do his best to stop them.'

Joseph's expression grew thoughtful.

'Thank you,' he said quietly. 'You've been most helpful. Perhaps you could have some food brought up for us?'

Lucy caught the glimmer of a gold coin. This time it was the turn of the landlord to grow animated.

'Yes, sir. Right away, sir.'

And away he bustled, leaving behind the weary group. Joseph's money had clearly done the trick. Much sooner than Lucy had dared expect, an entire chicken was sent up to them along with bread and boiled potatoes — the sort of feast they had not been able to enjoy since leaving the farm.

The children ate heartily, but were too small to make much headway with the chicken, so the adults could eat their fill without feeling they were depriving the little ones. But while the women and children chattered cheerfully, their spirits raised by their improved circumstances, Lucy noticed that Joseph seemed preoccupied. Throughout the meal, he hardly spoke a word.

Once supper was over, he slapped his knees suddenly and hauled himself to his feet.

'It might be as well to obtain more information about the whereabouts of the British ships,' he said. 'I'll go and see what I can overhear in the taproom while you put the children to bed.'

This was no easy task, since the children were now revived and excited. Nor, despite persistently ringing the bell, could they get anyone to come upstairs and bring them some hot water. In the end, Lucy lost her patience.

'I'll go myself,' she said.

The taproom was still thronged and some of the rougher men seemed the worse for drink, but Lucy pushed down her fear and plunged into the melee. She was not surprised none of the servants had answered the bell. They seemed rushed off their feet as it was.

Eventually she managed to catch one of the barmaids in passing and gave her the message. The maid promised to see to it straightaway and with a sigh of relief, Lucy turned to fight her way back to the stairs. She had nearly reached them when she was arrested by a familiar voice.

'How long would it take to get there by boat?'

Lucy pricked up her ears. From where she stood, she could only see Joseph's tricorn above the high back of an old-fashioned settle. His companion — whoever he was — was wholly invisible.

The other man sucked his teeth.

'Best part of the night, I shouldn't wonder,' a guttural voice replied, 'even with the current and the wind in our favour. That's as long as they haven't moved from their last mooring. But it's a risky business, by night or by day.'

'You'll be well paid.'

Lucy had never heard Joseph's voice sound so hard and it made her shiver.

'How well?'

She heard a coin being laid on the surface of the table and slid across to the other man.

'I'll double that if I get there safely.'

The stranger uttered a low whistle. Lucy felt a jolt of lightning pass through her. If I get there safely? Why was he using the singular and not the plural? Surely he was not intending to leave his travelling companions behind?

She missed the next words, which were spoken more softly than the previous ones.

'Half an hour,' the gruff stranger said, rising so Lucy caught a glimpse of a weather-beaten face in the demonic light of a nearby candle.

He moved away, apparently without noticing Lucy, who had instinctively drawn into the shadows. Her mind was still working furiously, trying to make sense of what she had overheard.

Before she could decide what to do, Joseph rose. She took two steps forward and, at the sound, Joseph turned his head. She thought she saw a guilty look dart across his face. 'What are you doing here?' he asked.

'Never mind that. I heard you talking to that man. Just tell me — were you planning to abandon us here and go off on your own?'

8

It all suddenly made sense to Lucy —
Joseph's quietness at supper, his hasty
excuse to leave, his urging them to put
the children to bed. The thought of
being stranded so many miles from
home, without means of support, no
friends and precious little money, with
three children all under the age of
seven, made her feel sick with terror.

But even worse was the thought that
Joseph Selbourne, a man she had come
to trust, could do this to them. She felt
like she was falling and falling and
would never stop.

'Clearly you didn't hear quite enough,'
Joseph replied grimly. 'I was just about
to go to talk to you and Abigail.'

He took her by the arm and led her
upstairs. They found Abigail at her wits'
end, the two older children tucked up
in bed, but with eyes still popping open

with excitement, while their mother paced to and fro, trying to settle the baby.

'Abigail, I'm so sorry,' Joseph said without preamble. 'I had hoped we might be able to stay here for the night, but we'll have to get the children dressed again.'

Abigail stopped in the midst of her circuit to stare at him.

'What?' she demanded indignantly.

'We must go tonight, before the British ships have moved,' he went on in a rapid undertone. 'They might come further upriver, of course, but they might just as easily retreat — there's talk of mutiny among the pilots — and we'll never catch up with them if we don't leave now. This is our best hope of avoiding having to walk the whole way to the Hudson Highlands.'

Lucy and Abigail exchanged looks. They knew without being told that secrecy was paramount. In this strange place, they had no idea who was a friend and who might betray his or her suspicions that Joseph was an enemy spy to the local authorities, military or civilian.

Neither Jenny nor Robin was unduly upset at being allowed to get up and get dressed again, and the fact that all three adults insisted that they had to be quiet and only talk in whispers made the adventure even more exciting.

To avoid attracting attention, Joseph would only let them slip out singly, with one child each. Lucy went first with Jenny and was joined presently by Abigail with Caroline, while Joseph elected to go out through the kitchen to the stable-yard, as if Robin had asked to see the horses.

Joseph had clearly got directions from his drinking companion, since he led them confidently through the dark streets. Even before she saw it, Lucy could hear the river, its waves lapping against tethered boats and ships.

'Wait here,' Joseph breathed. 'I'll go and see if our boatman is about.'

Stomach clenched with dread, Lucy watched him vanish into the darkness. It had come as a huge relief that he had not planned to desert them, and yet she could not quite shake off her doubts. Suppose he simply disappeared now?

The low whistle they had agreed on as a signal seemed unnaturally loud in the dark. Irrationally afraid, Lucy hesitated a moment.

'Come on,' Abigail said, brushing past her with Robin clutching her hand.

Lucy gathered her courage as they groped their way forward. The river was almost as dark as its bank and none of them wanted any unfortunate accidents.

Suddenly a lantern flashed out in the darkness.

'Do you think that's our boat?' Lucy asked in a whisper.

'Let's hope so,' Abigail replied.

They heard angry whispers as they drew closer to the light.

'Nothing was said about taking more

than one person,' the boatman was saying.

'You'll be paid handsomely — I've already promised you that. And I'll help with the rowing too.'

Caroline, disturbed by the voices, uttered a cry.

'A baby?' the boatman demanded, catching sight of them at last. 'Are you mad?' His eyes took in Jenny and Robin too. 'Nothing was said to me about children.'

'They're well behaved and will do as they're told,' Joseph replied. 'Here, Lucy, pass me that knapsack.'

The boatman looked mutinous, but he did not prevent Joseph from lifting down their baggage, then offering his hand to Lucy to help her into the boat. The lantern light was inadequate and Lucy felt a jolt of fear as the boat rocked beneath her feet.

'Do you think you can climb over to the seat in the bow?' Joseph asked.

'I'll try,' she said.

But Joseph obviously was not satisfied with this reply and did not release her hand until she had clambered over all the half-hidden obstacles and seated herself. Then he lifted Jenny down and carried her to her aunt. Abigail, meanwhile, was seconding the boatman's arguments, urging that the night would be bitter and the children would suffer.

'Can we not at least wait until morning before we set out?'

'I'm sorry. Time is of the essence. I'm doing this for your own good.'

Jenny shivered in Lucy's embrace.

'Is Uncle Joseph cross with Mamma?' she whispered in Lucy's ear.

'No, no, they're not cross, just a little anxious,' Lucy replied. 'Don't worry — everything will turn out for the best, I'm sure it will. And isn't this an adventure? Much better than being sent to bed. Look at all those stars up there — that means there won't be any rain because there aren't any clouds . . . '

It also meant that it would be bitterly cold and that there might well be a frost before morning, but Lucy resolutely forbade herself from saying those words out loud.

While she had been trying to encourage Jenny, Joseph had helped Robin into the boat, followed by Abigail and the baby. Jenny uttered a smothered shriek when the boat rocked and water splashed upward, but Lucy covered her mouth with her hand.

'There's nothing to be scared of,' she said, but it was herself she was trying to reassure as much as the child.

Still grumbling to himself, the boatman cast off and took his place. Lucy heard the clatter of oars in the rowlocks and as they edged into the dark current, she closed her eyes and prayed that everything would turn out right.

* * *

Lucy had never known nights could be so long, or that she could feel so alone while so close to other people. But for their safety, conversation had to be kept to a minimum. Nor had she ever felt so cold in her life, despite her winter cloak and woollen gown. She had pulled her cloak around Jenny too, who had laid her heavy head in her aunt's lap.

Above the rush of the river and the dip and pull of the oars through the water, she could hear the thousand sounds of the forest at night — the hum of the breeze through the pines, the occasional cry of an owl, the scurry of some creature as it fled from the water's edge at the approach of the boat.

Caroline grizzled at intervals at the far end of the boat and Lucy had heard Robin whispering questions to his mother or Uncle Joseph. But after a while, he too fell silent and Lucy wondered if he had fallen asleep like Jenny and, presumably, Caroline.

Sleep for Lucy was impossible, however. She was too alert and in any case, there was nothing for her to lean against and no way in which she could make herself more comfortable. After a time, she realised her neck was growing stiff because her head was perpetually turned towards the east, hoping against hope that soon the first glimmers of morning would become visible.

Her eyes were sore and her head aching by the time dawn finally arrived in a creep of silver light that gradually turned gold. As the light grew, indistinct shapes took on more concrete forms. The huddled mass became once again Joseph, the boatman and, beyond them, Abigail, looking pale and red-eyed, with Robin drowsing uneasily, his head laid beside his younger sister.

Colour returned to the landscape, the dark greens of the conifers, the reds and golds of the other trees, especially the maples. In spite of herself, Lucy felt her heart lifting. Plagued by her aching feet while they had been trudging along, she had ceased to admire the beauty of the landscapes she was passing through. She was just beginning to enjoy herself when Abigail suddenly exclaimed.

'Look!'

Lucy craned her head over her

shoulder and involuntarily she drew in her breath. They were just rounding a bend in the river and as the trees parted, the prow of a ship appeared. Behind it, a whole forest of other masts rose, tall, stark and bare, like lightning-blasted pines, in the pale autumnal sky.

Jenny stirred and grunted vaguely in Lucy's lap, as if annoyed that her sleep had been disturbed by her mother's cry.

'This is it,' Joseph said, half to himself. 'We've made it in time.'

Lucy sensed he was bracing himself, because what happened next depended entirely on his eloquence. He tied a white handkerchief to one of the oars as an improvised flag.

'Steer towards the leading ship,' he said to the boatman.

The man did as he was bid, but before they had reached their target, a voice rang out across the stillness of the morning, demanding to know their identity and their business.

All three children stirred, Caroline in particular uttering an indignant cry.

Joseph rose to his feet.

'I'm Captain Joseph Selbourne, aide-de-camp to General Clinton. I've an important message for Major-General Vaughn.'

Peering up at the ship, Lucy could see the man on watch duty give Joseph an odd look, particularly as he noticed the women and children.

'What kind of message?' the sentry asked suspiciously.

'One that I can only deliver to the major-general himself,' Joseph replied, refusing to be browbeaten. 'I think you'll find he is familiar with my name and rank.'

The dryness of his tone made the sentry hesitate. Fortunately, the little exchange had attracted several more figures onto the deck — Lucy could not be sure from this oblique angle whether they were soldiers or sailors. At any rate, someone was dispatched to deliver the message.

Time dragged while they waited. Suppose the major-general doesn't allow us onto the ship, Lucy thought. Or suppose he insists that Joseph has to go aboard, but the rest of us must be left behind.

The boatman was looking distinctly uneasy. The current of the river was strong and he was having great difficulty controlling the boat so they wouldn't be carried too far away from what Lucy presumed was the flagship of the fleet.

At last the call came for them to approach. Joseph turned towards Lucy and she could see how grim he looked.

'You'll have to go first with Jenny,' he murmured barely audibly. 'Do you think you can manage?'

The closer they drew, the taller the ship became. Her petticoats and long cloak would impede her, even without being hampered by a half-asleep child. But she knew this was their best chance.

'I'll try,' she said, attempting a smile.

What it meant, of course, was ushering Jenny ahead of her, promising her that she would catch her if she stumbled. But as Lucy rose, assisted by Joseph, there was a protest from above.

'Not the women and children.'

Joseph shook his head. 'I'm not leaving them behind. They're under my protection — I've given them my oath as a gentleman.'

In spite of the combined mumblings of discontent, Joseph urged Jenny and Lucy on.

'I'll be right here to catch you if anything goes wrong,' he said.

'And remember, Jenny, we're Priors and that means we can do anything if we put our mind to it,' Lucy added.

Jenny did not look convinced, but with encouragement from Lucy and Joseph, she managed to clamber, rung by rung, up the ladder. The soldiers, perhaps impressed by the courage shown by such a young child, leaned over the bulwark to help her up the last section and then came to Lucy's aid. The latter found herself shaking from exertion, fear and exhilaration by the time she joined her niece on deck.

'There, Jenny, you see, we did it,' she said, though her voice wobbled a little. 'Your papa would be proud of you for being such a brave girl.'

But it was as much for her own comfort as for her niece's that Lucy hugged Jenny tightly. Since one woman and child were already on board, the sailors reluctantly consented to help Abigail and the younger children up. Their belongings were also hauled aboard and Joseph followed last of all, having paid off the boatman.

The Priors were left in a huddle on the deck, while Joseph was escorted to what Lucy assumed must be Vaughn's cabin to explain his presence there and to argue their case, so they would not be set ashore somewhere along the way.

It was disconcerting to be the object of so many curious stares from men in red soldiers' uniforms or the blue of sailors. Caroline was crying, hungry or wet, but Abigail could not tend her in such an exposed place.

It seemed hours before Joseph returned, this time without an escort.

'Well?' Lucy and Abigail spoke simultaneously.

Joseph's expression did not look encouraging and Lucy's heart sank. He dropped his chin on his breast.

'Major-General Vaughn has agreed to let you travel with us — extremely reluctantly, I might add,' he said. 'Indeed, the chief reason why he is permitting it is because the convoy has been ordered back to New York, since Howe wants reinforcements elsewhere and there is nothing to be gained by going onward, now Burgoyne has surrendered.'

'I hope you assured the major-general that we are all grateful,' Abigail said.

'I did, but I trust you will have an opportunity of telling him yourselves,' Joseph replied.

Lucy was surprised. She had taken it for granted that they would be regarded as too far beneath the notice of the commanding officer to have anything to do with him. Perhaps Joseph guessed what she was thinking since he went on: 'There's one more thing I must warn you about,' he said, scarce above a breath. 'I told General Vaughn that Lucy and I are engaged to be married.'

Lucy flushed scarlet. 'Why on earth did you tell him that?' she blurted out and instantly regretted sounding so appalled.

Joseph averted his face, but Lucy thought she glimpsed a hurt look in his eyes. 'Because of what happened to Jane McCrea,' he said.

'Jane McCrea?' Lucy echoed.

'You haven't heard? It's not a pretty story.' Joseph glanced at the children, who were watching him with bulging eyes. 'She was betrothed to one of the Loyalist officers under Burgoyne's command. He was worried about her safety and sent two Indian scouts to fetch her. Unfortunately they fell out amongst themselves and apparently killed and scalped her instead. The rebel newspapers were full of the story, claiming that civilians were not safe under British protection.'

Lucy shuddered and Abigail hastily shushed Jenny's piercingly loud question, 'What does 'scalped' mean?'

'In the circumstances, Vaughn couldn't say no,' Joseph continued. He cleared his throat. 'I just thought you ought to know.'

'Yes, of course,' Lucy said. Joseph began to turn, as if to leave them, and impulsively she caught him by the arm. 'You know we are all very grateful to you.' His eyes fixed on hers and for a heart-stopping moment, Lucy couldn't look away, almost, almost convinced that he was going to kiss her. Instead he smiled and brushed his hand against her wind-chapped cheek.

'Think nothing of it,' he said.

9

It was not without grumbling that the most junior officer on board was induced to give up his cramped cabin to the Priors. The bunk was scarcely wide enough for all five of them, even sleeping top to toe, with bundles of clothes instead of pillows and the children wedged against the wall so there would be no danger of them falling out. But the cabin was dry and warm, in comparison with the conditions they had grown used to.

Fortunately the only one among them who snored was Caroline and it was such a delicious little sound that Lucy didn't even mind when it kept her awake. She couldn't help wondering, though, if she would ever be lucky enough to have a baby of her own.

It took a while to get used to the motion of the ship, though the river was nowhere near as rough as the open sea would have been. In bright weather, the Priors could venture up onto the deck, as long as they did not get in the way, and the children soon recovered enough high spirits to play and squabble with each other.

There was much to admire in the scenery that slipped past them. In places steep cliffs towered above them and the river seemed to grow wider every day. Lucy shuddered to think how long it would have taken them to toil through these dense forests or scale those hills on foot. The journey that would have taken them weeks, perhaps months, was being compressed into a matter of days.

It turned out there was no shortage of food on the ship, something that had troubled both Lucy and Abigail because they knew that by rights neither they nor the children were entitled to army rations. But it seemed the fleet had been loaded up with stores of dried, salted and pickled food, intended for

Burgoyne's beleaguered troops.

Initially Lucy felt extremely awkward about her false engagement to Joseph and clearly he felt the same way. Fortunately their blushes were mistaken for those of bashful lovers being subjected to the glare of public scrutiny for the first time.

But after a few days, it became almost too easy to laugh at Joseph's stories and gaze at him when she thought nobody was watching. The gravest danger, Lucy kept reminding herself, was that she might take his tender looks or affectionate remarks too seriously. It was all pretence. And yet sometimes it felt very real.

For the first time in her life she and, by extension, Abigail, were elevated to the rank of ladies. They were invited to eat with the officers and those wives who had refused to be left behind in New York. Most treated them with scrupulous courtesy, despite their rough hands and work-worn clothes. There were only a few disdainful remarks and haughty looks, particularly from the ladies, but the situation was made bearable because there were two of them. So if Lucy ever began to feel as if nothing she did was good enough, Abigail would support and encourage her.

Joseph spent as much time with them as he could. He pointed out to them the forts the British had captured at the beginning of the month, from which he had set out on his doomed mission northwards.

'With the wind and the current in our favour, it won't be long now before we reach New York,' he added.

Lucy suppressed a sigh. Reaching New York would mean having to face new trials. It wouldn't be easy to find shelter and employment in the already overcrowded city. And then there was also the fact nobody had dared mention — that Joseph's duties would occupy most of his time and might even take him away from New York and into danger. This close friendship might fizzle out or be brought to an abrupt conclusion and she was not sure she could bear either possibility.

At nights, overheated, crowded and frequently kicked by one or other of the children, Lucy found herself lying awake for hours, thinking about Joseph, worrying about his safety and remembering his smiles and words and gestures.

But although she thought she was prepared for the journey's end, it still came as a shock when one of the officers remarked at dinner, 'At the rate we're progressing, we'll be in New York by noon tomorrow.'

Lucy had been laughing at one of Joseph's tales, but the overheard words were a dagger to her heart. The smile died instantly on her lips and she scarcely noticed Joseph's puzzled look at the sudden change of her expression.

The officer's words kept recurring to her and after she had helped Abigail put the children to bed, she slipped up onto the deck, whispering to her sister-in-law before she left that she had a headache and hoped a breath of air might do her good.

It was quiet on the deck at this hour and the wind was sharp enough to keep everyone indoors who was not compelled to be there by duty. Or so she had thought. She was just about to return to her cabin when two voices caught her ear. She turned away, not wanting to eavesdrop, when a familiar name attracted her attention.

'I don't mean to pry, Selbourne, but you do have your commanding officer's permission to marry Miss Prior, don't you?'

Lucy blinked, baffled. It had never occurred to her that a gentleman well past the age of twenty-one might need permission to marry from anyone. Joseph was obviously equally taken aback. Lucy heard him utter a laugh that could not disguise his unease.

'Why do you ask?'

'Why do you think? Selbourne, it's unfair of you to raise that poor girl's hopes so high if there is any chance Clinton might object to your choice of bride. Oh, she's pretty and plucky enough, I grant you, but is she really the right sort of girl to marry so far above her station?'

'I can see no objection to her,' Joseph replied stiffly. 'Miss Prior may not be a lady in the conventional sense, but she is courageous, generous and resourceful, and she is intelligent enough to learn any little refinements she may lack.'

'Yes, well, forgive me, but you are seeing her through a lover's eyes.'

Lucy's heart squeezed unbearably tight. She wanted to flee as the voices came closer, and yet there was a hideous fascination, which kept her rooted to the spot.

'I don't think you realise how much I owe Lucy Prior,' Joseph went on. 'She sheltered me when I was in danger of being captured and the whole of her family paid a terrible price for her impulsive act. It's possible her brother may be dead because of me.'

That possibility had lurked at the back of Lucy's mind, but she had never dared speak the words out loud, for fear of upsetting Abigail or the children.

'But is that any reason to marry the girl, or ruin your prospects for her sake? Why not make her your mistress instead? Nobody could possibly object to that.'

Lucy suddenly felt sick and dizzy. She had been raised to be respectable and regard marriage as her ultimate goal. But the officer's words had opened her eyes to the vast social gulf that separated her from Joseph.

'Mistress? No, it's out of the question. It would be rank ingratitude for me to ruin her as you suggest.'

Lucy could almost hear the other officer's indifferent shrug.

'I'm not suggesting you should seduce her and then abandon her in the streets. You could settle a small sum of money on her and . . . '

'Lucy would never consent to it and I

wouldn't even ask it of her. No, it's marriage or nothing, I'm afraid.'

Marriage or nothing. Lucy felt a momentary flare of joy, which died just as quickly as she remembered that their engagement was a sham.

Nothing. That was the hidden second meaning behind Joseph's words. She was nothing to him, except perhaps a friend.

But the other officer had not finished yet.

'Don't be so sure. If you broached the matter in the right way, you might be able to persuade her. I've seen how besotted she is with you.'

Lucy's cheeks burned crimson. She had thought her love was locked up so deep in her heart that not even Abigail had guessed how she felt. But now a virtual stranger had revealed her secret to Joseph, in the mistaken belief that he already knew.

'Is that really what you think?' Joseph asked slowly. Lucy realised that he had wanted to contradict the other man and then remembered he could not do so without exposing that he had lied about his engagement.

'Can you be in any doubt? It's obvious from the way she gazes at you.'

Too late, Lucy realised she ought to retreat. The pair of officers came into sight around the corner and both stuttered to a standstill as they recognised her. Lucy swallowed hard and backed away two steps before she murmured 'excuse me' and turned to flee.

'Lucy, wait.'

She plunged on regardless, but she had not quite reached the hatch down into the bowels of the ship, when somebody caught her by the sleeve.

'Please, Lucy, I have to talk to you.'

She was sure Joseph could hear how ragged her breathing was as she fought for self-control. She felt humiliated by the way in which the other officer had referred to her, as if she was a simple, lovesick girl whose feelings didn't matter.

'How much did you overhear?'

'Enough to know your friends think I am only good enough to become your — ' She could not bring herself to utter the word.

'That's not true. And even if it were, do you really think I would pay any attention to their opinions?'

His words soothed her a little, but her thoughts and feelings were still agitated. Joseph had taken hold of her hands and was chafing them between his own. Against her better judgement, she turned to face him. The darkness made her only more acutely aware of how close he was to her — and how much she wanted him to take her in his arms and kiss her.

'I have far too much respect for you ever to regard you in such a light. Indeed, I have grown — very fond of you over the last weeks . . . '

She stopped him before he could go any further. 'Please, don't say any more. I know what you're going to say.'

He wanted to let her down gently,

but she could not bear the thought that he felt sorry for her because he could not return her love.

Joseph drew in a deep breath. 'Very well. I swear I won't distress you by speaking of such things again. I knew Captain Dixon must be mistaken about your feelings for me. But — but we can still be friends, can't we? For the sake of the children?'

Lucy had to struggle with her feelings. She wanted to tell him that she could never be his friend again because seeing him and knowing he did not return her love would be simply too hard.

But for the sake of Abigail and the children, she could not say no. They needed a friend in the alien environment of New York. She nodded silently, not trusting her voice.

'You're shivering,' he said. 'I'd better let you go before you catch cold. Goodnight, Lucy.'

'Goodnight,' she murmured before fleeing.

Her breathing seemed very sharp and loud in the silence of the cabin as she leaned against the door. Abigail too had gone to bed and all she could hear was the creaking of timbers and the slap of waves against the hull of the ship.

Her chilled, stiff fingers made it difficult to undress. By some miracle, she hadn't woken anyone by the time she clambered into the bunk. She knew she wouldn't sleep, however. There was far too much to think about.

Lucy was no clearer in her mind when the next day dawned. She woke exhausted, having only slept patchily, tormented by her thoughts.

Fortunately there was much to do to get the children up and fed, and soon after that New York was sighted, so Lucy had to help Abigail pack the remainder of their belongings and make sure nothing was left behind in the cabin.

She had seen Joseph briefly at breakfast. She half-expected that there would be something different about his behaviour towards her after the incident the previous night, but he seemed to be more or less his usual self. If anything, he paid more attention to Abigail than normal and spoke to Lucy rather less.

Hurt, she drew back into herself and no one seemed to notice she was quieter than was her wont, perhaps because Jenny and Robin were both full of questions about what lay ahead of them. Lucy found herself stealing glances at Joseph, analysing every look and word he bestowed on her family, and her turmoil only increased. Once or twice she caught him watching her, but then she quickly broke their gaze.

During the night she had had a chance to remember how Joseph had defended her against Captain Dixon's slights and insinuations, and she realised now she had let her hopes rise unrealistically high as a result. But by Joseph's own admission, he was only 'very fond' of her, no more than that.

On the road, they had all been equals, enduring the same weather conditions, poor food and draughty lodgings, and she had allowed herself to forget that she belonged to the wrong social class. Her only consolation was that Joseph thought the other officer was mistaken about the extent of her feelings for him.

She still felt indignant about Captain Dixon's slurs, and yet she was uncomfortably aware that if Joseph tried to seduce her with smiles, kisses and kind words, she might well give way. Just the sound of his voice was enough to send ripples along her skin.

Their arrival in New York gave her other things to worry about. She had not been in a city since she was a little girl, when they had moved from Boston to the farm her father had worked on until his death.

She had forgotten how bustling and noisy harbours could be, with dozens, nay hundreds of voices shouting to try to make themselves heard. Jenny and

Robin clung to her skirts or their mother's, terrified of being lost or left behind. Neither of them had ever been in a port before and in their eyes everything was new; exciting and frightening at the same time.

Lucy was apprehensive herself. This was, after all, a completely strange place to her and to Abigail. They didn't know a single soul there, apart from Joseph, and no doubt he would have his own duties to carry out once they had all set foot on dry land.

Lucy glanced at Abigail. She too was looking very pale and determined, clearly as frightened as her sister-in-law, but resolved not to show it in front of the children.

Disembarking seemed a chaotic process to Lucy, but she guessed there must be method behind the apparent madness. Fortunately Joseph appeared just in time to assist them into an overcrowded boat that took them ashore.

Lucy felt a tingle run along her arm

and through her whole body as Joseph grasped her hand to help her clamber onto the steps that led up to the quay. He smiled as his eyes met hers.

'Welcome to New York,' he said.

10

'I'm sorry I'm late,' Lucy said as she struggled in through the door of the cramped garret she shared with her family.

It was March and the Priors had been in New York for more than four months now.

'Here, let me help you with that,' a deep voice said.

Lucy gasped as the heavy basket of groceries was taken effortlessly out of her grip and placed on the table. The red coat told her instantly who their guest was, and yet she had to look up at his face, for fear she was mistaken.

She smiled and thanked Joseph, but an unexpected wave of shyness washed over her. The situation between them had been awkward ever since that last night on the ship, despite their attempts to ignore what had happened. She had battled hard to conquer her feelings for him over the last months, to no avail. Every act of generosity Joseph displayed towards her family only made her love him more.

It had not been easy obtaining food during the harsh winter, but he had helped when he could. Once he had even brought them a bolt of linen to make new shifts, shirts and caps for the children. He had also recommended Lucy and Abigail as seamstresses and laundresses to his fellow officers and their wives, so they could earn a little cash.

'Uncle Joseph says he has news,' Jenny announced importantly. She was perched on a stool, helping her mother by painstakingly peeling the shell off one of the precious hard-boiled eggs Joseph had brought them.

'About Robert?' Lucy asked, her face lighting up as she looked up at their visitor. But her hopes died at his grave expression.

'No, I'm afraid not.'

Dishes clattered as Abigail methodically unpacked Lucy's purchases from the basket. Her face was closed and Lucy could have bitten her tongue. Why could she not have kept herself in check? She knew how hard it must be for Abigail, and yet she had spoken thoughtlessly, ripping open an unhealed wound.

There was every possibility that Robert was dead — executed or ill-treated by his captors, or sent off to fight a war he did not believe in, or the victim of one of the diseases that flourished in any prison.

Joseph cleared his throat.

'It's not good news, I'm afraid,' he said. 'I came to say farewell.'

Lucy froze, feeling as if a dagger of ice had been plunged into her heart.

'Farewell?' she echoed.

'General Clinton is preparing to leave for Philadelphia and as a member of his staff, I am obliged to accompany him.'

'Oh, but . . . ' Lucy croaked, not

really knowing what protest she wanted to make.

While Burgoyne had suffered a crippling defeat in the north, General Howe had been far more successful in outmanoeuvring Washington to seize Philadelphia, the largest and politically most important city in the whole of North America.

Joseph was still speaking, but Lucy hardly heard a word. All she knew was that her family was losing their last male protector and that they would be solely reliant on themselves if any crisis occurred.

But worse, far worse was the thought of being separated from Joseph. She knew enough about the perils of war by now to know that anything could happen to him on his way to or from Philadelphia or during his stay there. The remnants of General Washington's army were not far from Philadelphia, camped out in some isolated place whose name escaped her for the moment — Valley Forge?

Only two Christmases ago, Washington had taken everyone by surprise by crossing the ice-filled Delaware and all but obliterating some of the more unwary German regiments at Trenton. She didn't know enough about war to be sure that nothing like that would happen again.

'How long will you be gone?' Lucy asked hollowly.

'I've no idea.'

'But you'll stay and dine with us, won't you?' Abigail urged.

Joseph shook his head. 'I'm sorry. I have to attend an official dinner with one of my superiors, though I would be infinitely happier here. I was only waiting for Lucy to return before I left.'

Lucy closed her eyes. At every word, she felt more and more sick. She couldn't utter a sound.

'We'll all miss you,' Abigail said. 'Won't we, children?'

Jenny pouted. 'It's not fair. Why do you have to go away? Why can't you stay here with us?'

Joseph glanced down at the little girl, who had jumped down from her stool to cling to one of his legs. Robin, not to be outdone, grabbed his other leg and Caroline — who had grown most rapidly and visibly of all the children in the last months and was beginning to take a few shaky steps — looked as if she might join in too, though naturally she was too young to understand what strange game her brother and sister were playing with Uncle Joseph.

'I'll miss all of you too,' he said, placing one hand on each of the children's heads, 'but I promise I'll come back. Now, before I go, how about a kiss?'

He crouched down, with the result that the children clung round his neck instead. Caroline decided that this was a game she could definitely take part in and elbowed her way between her siblings.

Abigail allowed Joseph to whisper a few words to the children before she began untangling him from the mass of small arms. Belatedly Lucy stepped forward to scoop Caroline up onto her hip.

'Well, goodbye, Abigail,' Joseph said a little awkwardly as he straightened up. Then he leaned closer and pecked her hastily on the cheek before he turned towards Lucy.

Her throat was too full to allow her to speak, but she blinked back her tears. As she lifted her head, she realised Joseph was gazing deep into her eyes.

That gaze seemed to last for hours. She saw his face come closer and closer and she waited breathlessly, knowing he was going to kiss her, but not knowing which cheek he would choose.

She was afraid to move, afraid she would get it wrong, or move too soon, or spoil the moment somehow so he would pull back without kissing her at all.

And then his face came too close. Her vision blurred and she felt the warmth of his lips against her own.

She was too stunned to react and

when she did, it was too late. He drew back, away from her belated kiss. His hand reached out to stroke Caroline's downy cheek one last time, but his gaze never left Lucy's face.

'Goodbye, Lucy,' he murmured.

She couldn't move. In a moment he had whisked away. The room reverberated with his hurried footsteps on the stairs. Every impulse in Lucy's body told her to run after him, though she did not know what she would say or do if she did catch up with him.

Like a sleepwalker, she staggered towards the door, but deep down she knew it was too late. From a distance she could hear the children's voices. They had scampered across to the window, apparently unaware of the momentousness of what had just happened.

Lucy tottered across to join them. The window looked down into the street and just as she reached it, she heard the street door open and close beneath. And then the well-beloved figure in the red coat and black tricorn came into sight.

While she was gazing down at him, desperate longing in her eyes, he tilted his head upward, as if he had read her mind. Their eyes met for another moment, then he saluted smartly in reply to the children's waves before he turned on his heel and marched swiftly away.

Hours, days, weeks dragged by. Lucy had never realised how much they had all come to rely on Joseph. Even the children frequently brought themselves up short in the midst of saying something like 'Wait till Uncle Joseph hears this.'

Not that Lucy had much time to mope. Most of her waking hours were spent helping Abigail to take care of the children, cleaning their lodgings, sewing, washing, delivering finished goods, collecting new commissions, dunning clients for money that was owed them or buying groceries for the family.

It was only at night that she would lie awake, listening to the slow breathing of the others and going over in her mind every minute she had ever spent with Joseph since that first morning when he had startled her in the byre. It seemed such a long time ago now.

But most of all, Lucy thought about that last brief kiss. Why had he kissed her on the lips and not on the cheek, as he had with Abigail? Did it mean anything or not? If she thought hard enough, she could almost, almost feel it again tingling on her lips.

It didn't help that the children were anxious in case Uncle Joseph, like Papa, would never come back. The thought preyed a good deal on Lucy's mind, particularly as she trudged through the streets. New York was still full of British soldiers and every time she caught a glimpse of a red coat, her heart jumped painfully, hoping against hope that Joseph might have been sent back on some mission.

Scarcely a week after Clinton's departure, a letter arrived from London, announcing that he was to replace Sir William Howe as Commander-in-Chief and that Philadelphia was to be evacuated as part of a retrenching process, now that it looked as if the French and Spanish were about to be lured into the war by the Americans. Howe returned to New York before sailing for England. But after that weeks passed and nothing else happened.

March became April, April became May, May became June. After a brief burst of spring, summer arrived in an intense haze of heat that brought out all the smells of rotting from the rubbish-strewn streets. Diseases flourished, particularly in the poorer parts of town, which made Abigail worry about the children.

Lucy was on her way back from calling on a customer one hot afternoon towards the end of June when she became aware of a bustle in the streets. Usually, she did everything she could to avoid crowds and anything that smacked of unrest among the populace, but this time as she hurried on, she overheard something that made her stop.

'A whole fleet of them — back from Philadelphia, so I heard.'

The crowds seemed to be moving towards the harbour and, against her better judgement, Lucy found herself following. Sure enough, when she reached the quayside, she could see the prow of the foremost ship and the masts of several others behind it.

Her heart leapt in relief. Joseph was back, safe and well, as far as she knew. And yet she could not help having misgivings. Suppose the rumours were wrong. Suppose the ships were from England or Quebec instead.

She looked around and chose the most friendly-looking person she could see in her vicinity, an elderly man with a round, contented face.

'What is it?' she asked. 'Do you know? Are they from Philadelphia?'

'So they say,' he replied, taking his clay pipe out of his mouth. 'Mostly civilians, though, I believe. Women, children, Loyalists and the sick and wounded.'

Lucy's heart plummeted.

'Not the soldiers then?' she quavered.

'Haven't you heard? There weren't enough transports for them all. They're coming overland instead.' He grinned, obviously drawing his own conclusions from her crestfallen face. 'Got a sweetheart amongst them, eh?'

She managed a pale smile, but instead of confirming or denying his conjecture, she thanked him for the information and turned for home.

★　★　★

Lucy was tired and sunk in gloom by the time she reached their lodgings. She was oppressed by the thought that Joseph was more than likely on the march somewhere with the other redcoats, crossing who knew what wildernesses in the sweltering heat, with Continental regulars and militia threatening to attack at any moment. She had heard the men in the streets talking of such things as she passed, though she had tried to block her ears.

She took a deep breath before opening the door. She must not let Abigail or the children see that she was worried. She would only tell them that some evacuees had arrived from Philadelphia and that the rest were on their way.

Raising her head, she entered the room, her opening words already on her lips. But they froze there as she took in the scene.

The room was usually a hive of activity, with the children playing or helping out or the older two practising their ABC, while Abigail bustled about. But this time there was absolute stillness.

Abigail was sitting on the edge of the bed, a squirming Caroline on her lap. Robin was standing beside his mother, clutching her sleeve and watching her with huge eyes. Jenny was kneeling on the bed on the other side of her mother, her eyes also fixed on Abigail's face.

Abigail held a piece of paper in her trembling hand. Her head was lowered, but as she lifted her eyes, Lucy saw they were full of tears.

Joseph. Someone's written to say something has happened to Joseph. The conviction darted, lightning-swift, through Lucy's heart.

'What is it, Abigail? What's happened?'

She choked and could not go on. Caroline slid down from her mother's lap and began to totter towards her aunt.

'Oh, Lucy,' Abigail said. 'It's — it's from Robert. He's safe in Quebec — he managed to escape — and I've never been so happy in my life.' And then she burst into tears, much to the consternation of the older children, who hugged her from either side and begged her not to cry.

Lucy scooped up Caroline and flew across the room. She squashed onto the bed with the others, so she could squeeze as many of them in her embrace as possible.

'That's wonderful,' she said. 'I know everything will turn out perfectly now.'

And she was glad that her brother was safe and that somehow it might be possible for the family to be reunited. Yet she could not shake that nagging worry about Joseph. But she wouldn't burden Abigail with that now.

'I think we ought to have a celebration,' she said. 'Come on, children, let's go and see what we can find in the cupboards.'

★ ★ ★

Later Abigail gave Lucy the letter to read, since it was addressed to both of them. From it she discovered that Robert had decided ultimately that discretion was the better part of valour and, when no concrete evidence against him could be found, he had allowed himself to be enlisted in the Continental Army.

There he had bided his time until he found the perfect opportunity to desert. He headed northwards and after a long, exhausting and perilous journey, which he would tell them about when they were finally reunited, he had found his way to Quebec, where he had put himself under the protection of Sir Guy Carleton, the good-natured Governor of Canada.

From Quebec he had written to the farm and had grown increasingly desperate at the lack of a reply. Reading between the lines, Lucy suspected he had at times been tempted to retrace his journey across vast lakes, steep mountains and dense forests to discover what had become of his family.

At last a package had arrived from Mrs Goodall, enclosing the letter Lucy had left with her. Naturally, not knowing of the existence of Joseph, Robert had been extremely anxious about the safety of his family when he heard about their journey southwards. He had used every contact he had made in his short time in Quebec to try to get news from New York.

Fortunately, unbeknown to Lucy or Abigail, Joseph had been making enquiries about the whereabouts of Robert using his rather more extensive contacts and so eventually Robert had obtained an address in New York, to which he had sent this letter, hoping that it would reach its intended recipients.

The remainder of the letter was a series of questions, about their welfare, their journey to New York and so forth. The letter concluded with a million, million best wishes, kisses and prayers for their well-being.

Lucy found herself smiling secretly at Robert's questions about the identity of the mysterious Captain Selbourne who seemed to be taking such an interest in his family. It made her feel a little closer to Joseph, knowing that he had been working on their behalf behind their backs.

Please God, bring him back safely to New York, so I can thank him for all he has done for us, she prayed silently. I miss him so much.

Within days of receiving Robert's letter, their joy was adulterated by anxiety. It was Abigail who brought the news home this time, Lucy having been the one who stayed behind to take care of the children. Abigail looked grim as she entered the garret, though she replied to the children's questions calmly enough, if beside the point.

Lucy waited till later before she drew Abigail aside to find out more.

'Apparently the transports have just left the harbour for Sandy Hook to collect Clinton's army,' Abigail replied.

Lucy found a smile creeping across her face.

'But that's good news, isn't it?' she asked. 'It means Joseph will be back soon. Doesn't it?'

Her voice quavered in spite of herself

on the last words. There was something unsettling about the compassionate way in which Abigail was watching her.

Sandy Hook was not very far, only on the other side of the bay. There was no need even to venture out into the ocean and encounter all the risks that that entailed. But there was another nagging fear in Lucy's heart, which Abigail's next words confirmed.

'I'm sorry, Lucy. They're saying there's been a battle at some place called' — she furrowed her brow, trying to remember — 'Monmouth Court-house, I think it was. Nobody knows as yet how many were killed or anything else about it, and there's no saying that Joseph was directly involved, but — but I thought it might be better to warn you.'

Lucy felt all the blood drain from her face and she knew from the way Abigail was watching her that her sister-in-law was afraid she might faint.

All her worst fears had been realised, but she could not give way now. She would cry only when she knew the worst. With an effort she swallowed her tears and flung her arms around Abigail.

'Don't worry about me,' she said, squeezing her sister-in-law tightly. 'I'll cope, whatever happens.' Again her voice shook, but she forced herself to go on. 'Thank you for telling me.'

'Oh, Lucy, you don't have to be so brave all the time. I know how much you care for Joseph. I've seen it in your eyes.'

Oh dear, Lucy thought as her eyes filled up. Here come the waterworks after all.

★ ★ ★

After that, Lucy took to haunting the quayside whenever she could get away from her duties. It was fortunate for her that other soldiers' wives and sweethearts did the same because otherwise she was sure she would have been mistaken for a streetwalker, despite her otherwise respectable appearance.

The walking wounded were the first to be brought ashore, along with those soldiers' wives who had been authorised to join the march, or had done so without permission. From them Lucy discovered that the more severely injured men had been left behind with a surgeon under a flag of truce, in the hopes of receiving merciful treatment from the Americans.

She also heard more disturbing tales, of a battle waged in three narrow defiles between hills, of sweltering heat and men dropping dead of heatstroke under the weight of their packs and thick red coats. Technically the battle was a British victory, but the cost had been severe on both sides.

The evacuation took several days and as it was taking place, there was still a danger that the smaller and smaller group of soldiers left behind on the opposite shore could be attacked by far superior numbers of Continental troops.

By far the biggest difficulty Lucy faced was the sheer number of men being brought back to New York, not only British soldiers, but also some of the hired Hessian troops. Since Lucy could not spend every waking moment by the docks, there was every chance that she would not be present when Joseph returned, or that even if she was there, she would not spot him in the crowd.

Weary after one such vigil, Lucy finally turned for home. It was getting late and it was none too safe for a solitary female to be out at this hour.

And then suddenly she heard his voice.

'Lucy!'

She turned, her heart thudding. It wasn't the first time she had thought she caught his particular accent, nor the first time she had heard her name, only to find that the speaker was calling somebody else who shared her name, or even shouting some completely different name altogether — Betsy or Nancy or Sally.

And then among the bobbing heads, broad shoulders and high-piled knap-sacks, she saw him on the opposite side of the street. She was running before she could stop herself, dodging and ducking between the people that interposed themselves between her and her goal.

A minute later, a strong pair of arms had wrapped around her and lifted her a good foot off the ground so she was forced to snatch hold of Joseph's shoulders, terrified that he would drop her.

'Oh, thank God, you're safe,' she gasped. 'You're not hurt or sick, or anything?' She ran her eyes over his face, afraid she had missed something.

'No, no, there's nothing wrong with me that this cannot cure,' Joseph murmured and before she had time to catch her breath, he was kissing her hungrily upon the lips.

'Joseph,' she gasped, as he let her slide down his body till her feet touched the ground. She felt as dizzy as if she was about to faint.

She was being buffeted by the crowd, pushed closer against Joseph's breast, and she felt both protected and vulnerable because of the number of people there. She knew it was wrong to allow Joseph to kiss her like that in a public place; on the other hand, everyone seemed so intent on their own business, there was a good chance nobody had even noticed them.

'I'm sorry. I lost control. But you must know how I feel. These months away have been agony. Please, Lucy, won't you reconsider and — and marry me?'

'M-marry you?' Lucy flushed. 'But I thought . . . ' She felt as if the ground had gone from under her as she remembered the scene on board ship on the night before they reached New York.

Had Joseph been trying to propose to her when she cut him short? Dear God, how many months she had wasted, torturing them both because she hadn't realised what he intended to say . . .

'Lucy?' Joseph's voice broke through her confused thoughts. He drew in a long, shuddering breath, as if trying to steady his nerves. 'Oh God, you hate the idea, don't you? You love me as a brother and not . . . '

'I love you with my heart and soul. But I never thought you could possibly return my feelings.'

Even as she uttered the breathless words, another vivid memory flashed across her mind. Joseph smiled incredulously as he drew her closer, but Lucy pushed against his breast with both hands, trying to create some distance between them.

'Is it true that you have to ask your superiors for permission to marry?'

A slight frown darkened Joseph's brow.

'Yes, it's true,' he said, 'but no one will be able to deny you have the courage to endure the hardships of a soldier's wife, after all the trials we shared on our journey. So all we have to do is reassure my superiors that you are refined enough to hold your own in more genteel society.'

Lucy glanced down at her homespun gown, which looked distinctly the worse for wear. The hands that still rested on his breast were red and hard. She could read and write and do plain sewing, but all the other accomplishments of a lady were well beyond her.

'Perhaps this isn't such a good idea,' she said slowly, drawing back still further. But her heart squeezed into a fist as she realised the only alternative meant renouncing Joseph forever.

She could sense his eyes on her face, even without looking up.

'I won't deny it will be hard,' he said softly, 'but I had hoped that you loved me enough to want to overcome this barrier rather than give way before it.'

She had hurt him. She could hear it in his voice, though he tried to hide it. His arms slid away from around her waist and her eyes flew up to his face just as he averted it. She couldn't let him go so easily and instinctively, she grabbed his arm.

'I do love you,' she said, feeling a gush of colour in her cheeks as she uttered the words. 'It's just that I'm afraid that I might try and try and still not be good enough and then — and then giving you up would be so much harder . . . ' Her last words disintegrated under the pressure of incipient tears.

Her vision blurred and suddenly Joseph's left arm was wrapped round her again while his other hand gently brushed her tears away.

'You won't fail, Lucy,' he said. 'I'll help you any and every way I can. And if my superiors are too narrow-minded to see you would be an asset to the British Army, well — then I'll resign my commission.'

'Oh, but you can't,' she stammered.

'I can and I will, if that is the only way to keep you. I cannot imagine living without you.'

Warmth spread through her body.

She felt overwhelmed that any man could love her enough to sacrifice a promising career for her sake.

'Oh, Joseph,' she murmured, tentatively allowing her hands to creep up his arms to his shoulders. 'I won't disappoint you — I promise.'

A smile of joy and relief crept across Joseph's face.

'Then you will marry me?' he asked.

Silently Lucy nodded, her throat suddenly too full for speech. Joseph dipped his head to kiss her, long and lingeringly, on the lips.

'You won't regret this,' he said. 'Now let's go and tell Abigail and the children before you change your mind.'

THE END